Tonya Clark

CHAPTER ONE

CAMMIE

You know that saying, "This seems too good to be true?" Well, I have been telling myself just that since the holidays.

I wasn't expecting when I went home this past November for Thanksgiving that I would be offered what I would consider a "dream job." What was even crazier about the situation was that I still had six months to go before graduation at that time. Lucas, my best friend since grade school, mentioned a guy he knew was looking for a personal medic/sports trainer for his son who was a professional rider. In Texas, professional rider means bull rider, and what true country girl wouldn't be excited to work with a professional bull rider? I won't lie, I wanted to jump up and down like little girl and yell, "Yes, yes, yes!" but instead I took a very deep breath and asked, like any professional adult, for him to get me a little more information on the job.

For the couple of weeks between being home for Thanksgiving and returning home once again for Christmas, I hadn't heard from Lucas. I figured the job offer was no longer open. The first night home, Lucas came over. Entering in the door, there was no, "Hello, welcome home," or, "I missed you," it was, "You got the job." I was dumbfounded, how many people can say they are coming out of graduation with their dream job?

Now here I am, graduation over, the real world starting. My first day on the job and I'm still waiting for the bomb to drop. I haven't personally met the guy I will be working for. The gentleman who hired me took Lucas's word about me and I have only received a short email from him asking when I can start and requesting a list of equipment and supplies I will need. Again, "too good to be true." I trust Lucas, so I go against my better judgment and decide to roll with it and just be grateful.

ONE RING! Looking around, I'm thinking I should have taken Lucas up on his offer on coming with me today to introduce me to Mr. Maddox. I'm starting to think Lucas sent me the wrong place.

Before today, I attempted to do a little research of my own and look up professional riders with the last name Maddox, but none came up. I don't know why I didn't ask for more information about the rider I will be working with, but all of my communication, the little there was, went through Mr. Maddox, the father.

Two rings! "Come on, Lucas, answer your phone." All around me is dirt, but it's not an arena with corrals, and it definitely doesn't smell of bulls, which are two signs that I must be in the wrong place. This is some kind of track, with jumps of all sizes, I'm thinking a dirt bike track.

Three rings! He isn't answering, great! First day on the job and I'm going to be late because my idiot of a best friend gave me the wrong address.

"Are you Camille?" a voice comes from behind me. Lucas's phone goes to voicemail.

Now I'm really confused. If I'm not in the right location, how does anyone around here know my name? Shoving my phone into my back pocket, I turn to find a guy probably in his mid-fifties, I would guess.

"Young lady, if you are a reporter, then I will have to kindly ask you to leave."

I shake my head, not only to answer his question about being a reporter but also to clear my own head. I'm confused.

"Then I'm going to assume you are Camille Mitchell, our new medical personnel." He takes a couple steps toward me, his hand extended out to me. "I'm Michael Maddox."

Shaking his hand, I decide I better stop looking at him like an idiot. "I go by Cammie, but I'll be honest, Mr. Maddox, I'm a little confused. Lucas said I would be working with a professional rider."

Laughing, he looks around with pride in his eyes. "That's correct, my son, Kade Maddox."

Here is the "too good to be true" part. The bomb I've been waiting for. "Sir, no disrespect but this isn't an arena. We live in Texas, most 'professional riders' fall into the category of bull riding."

"I was wondering if Lucas gave you any details, Ms. Mitchell. I'm sorry if there has been any confusion, but Kade isn't a professional bull rider, my son is a professional motocross rider. Motorcycles, not bulls. I assure you no less dangerous. We are in need of medical staff on our team and you came very highly recommended by Lucas. I figured if he trusted that you could handle the job, then so could we."

How does Lucas know this family? For them to be taking his word on my ability, he must know them pretty well. I will have to ask Lucas that, along with many other questions, later. It's probably not fair to be blaming only Lucas for my confusion, I should have asked more questions. The last few months of school were so crazy with finals and all, I just answered emails sent to me and was just excited to be offered such an amazing opportunity. "Sir, I'm not saying the danger level isn't the same. I'm sorry if you think I'm disrespecting this profession, I'm just a little shocked is all."

I need to get over the disappointment, he may not be a bull rider, but this is still a really good opportunity for me. I don't need to screw it up. I would just like to know why Lucas thought he needed to mislead me into believing I was working with a bull rider for me to agree to the job.

Laughing slightly, Mr. Maddox shakes his head. "Ms. Mitchell, relax, I don't believe you're trying to disrespect what we do. I can see where you may have thought Kade was a bull rider. We do live in Texas," he repeats my earlier comment. "I should have given a little more detail to the job, it's been a little crazy. I just wanted to make sure we had everything ready for when you were able to start. We are a smaller race team, only two riders, but we like it that way. Kade is number two right now and is looking very promising to become number one this season in the four-fifty riders. Then we have Cody Ramson, our two-fifty rider who is running number three in his division. This has been a great season for us."

Four-fifty, two-fifty, I have absolutely no idea what he is talking about. Maybe this isn't going to work. "Mr. Maddox..."

"Please, call me Michael," he corrects me.

"Michael," I correct myself, "I'm going to be honest with you. I know nothing about motorcycle racing."

"Ms. Mitchell..."

"Cammie, please," it's my turn to correct him.

His smile is soft. "Cammie, I'm not really worried about what you know about racing, as long as you know how to fix them if they are to get hurt."

That I can do! Looking over at the track once more, I take a deep breath, probably my first one since leaving the house this morning. "Is there a big demand for medical personnel on these teams?" I ask over my shoulder.

Michael walks up to stand next to me. "Cammie, this sport is not only hard on the body with each jump landed and the strain in the muscles to control the machine you are on, there are also the crashes when another rider takes you out, or you land one of those jumps wrong and end up eating some dirt. The possibilities for injuries are endless on these tracks."

"There aren't medics during the races?" Why do I feel like I'm trying to talk this man out of hiring me with these questions? I should just thank my lucky stars that I have this opportunity and ask where he needs me to start setting up the stuff I brought.

"Of course there is medical personnel on site during races, but we want someone who gets to know the boys. Plus, they don't only get hurt or pull something during races, we practice for hours every day, we want someone on call at all times, making sure the boys are at 'tip-top shape' I guess you can say. Bringing in different people to work on the boys after each practice is getting harder. I would rather have someone on the payroll full-time." Michael turns to look down at me. "Cammie, when I say full-time that's what I mean, I need someone who doesn't ignore the call on their day off."

"So what you are saying is this is a twenty-four hour, seven days a week kind of thing," I want to clarify. I'm not afraid of a little hard work. This is a big job, I'm getting that now. I know I'm going to have to work hard.

Again, there is that soft smile. Strange how someone so large can smile so tenderly. "Actually, we run practices Monday through Friday, we arrive here, or our other training location, around eight in the morning and our days usually end around eight at night. We don't schedule training on the weekends so you will have that time off, unless we are at a race of course. Now what I mean by on call is, both boys are pretty determined to hit number one this season, so they don't understand a day of rest. You may receive a call on the weekend."

Monday through Friday and weekends, well, maybe the weekends, doesn't sound bad. This is really a no-brainer, why wouldn't I want to do this? So far, nothing this man has said has inched me in the direction of not wanting the job. Sure, I may not be very educated in the sport, but an injury or pulled muscle is the same no matter what sport you are doing. My job here is not going to be based on the sport, it's based on my knowledge of how to keep these "riders" in the best shape they can be in to do the sport they are involved with, regardless if that's a bull or a bike.

"So, Cammie, can I officially welcome you to our team?" Michael's voice breaks through my thoughts.

I look down at his extended hand, but before I can answer a voice booms through the air.

"I thought we weren't talking to the press, Dad." The strong voice comes from behind us.

A chill runs up my body and goosebumps shoot across my skin. What the hell is that about? Michael turns around next to me but for some odd reason my feet aren't moving. What is wrong with me?

"Kade, this isn't a reporter, this is Cammie, our new medical personnel?" Michael is now eyeing at me with a look of uncertainty on his face. He is waiting on me to give him my answer.

Well, first I need to find my feet and turn around. I want to slap myself in the face but I'm sure that would just send the message to these two men that I may be crazy. Turning around, there goes that chill again, oh holy riders! When someone asks me my type of guy, one word usually can answer that question—cowboy! The guy standing in front of me right now is far from cowboy. He has to be taller than six feet and built nicely. He has strong arms, I can see them through the riding jersey he is wearing. No cowboy boots, instead he has on riding boots, and he is carrying a helmet in one hand at his side. His sandy-blond hair is shaved up short on the sides, a little longer and messy on top. I find myself rubbing my fingers against my palms, my hands itch to run through it. Then there are the eyes, a green I have never seen before. Almost an emerald green, very bright, I could swear he can see right through me and all my thoughts, especially with that cocky grin he is giving me right now.

Everything cools inside me the moment I realize there is someone standing next to him. His arm is draped around the shoulders of a girl who doesn't look to me to be any older than maybe eighteen. She is a red head, very low-cut top on, her breasts high and on display for all to see. If her shorts were any shorter she wouldn't really need to be wearing them. Then there are the heels. Really, surrounded by all this dirt, high heels seemed a good idea? Of course she doesn't look like someone who gets dirty, well at least not dirt, dusty dirty.

If this is the type of woman he goes after, that cools any fire that shot through me at first sight. Sure, he is good-looking, but he is also cocky, I can see it in his eyes, he knows he's good.

I extend my hand out to Kade. "Hello, Kade, it's nice to meet you. I'm Cammie."

He looks me up and down slowly. I'm dressed simply compared to his friend who is hanging onto him a little tighter right now. Jeans, my cowboy boots, which are part of my daily wardrobe, and a simple white button-down shirt.

"Do you know anything about motocross, or motorcycles at all?" His eyes challenge me with his question, and the girl smiles smugly.

I can guarantee that girl doesn't know the first thing about what goes on here, she is just after the riders. "I can assure you that my knowledge to be able to do my job here is well above sufficient."

His low chuckle hits me right in my core. What the hell is wrong with me? I don't even want to be this man's type if the woman hanging on him is any indication of what that type is.

"We will see." He looks me over one more time, then turns and walks away. He whispers something in the red-head's ear and her giggle causes me to roll my eyes.

"So I'm going to assume that this means you are good with working with us here?" Michael's voice breaks through my thoughts and I realize I'm staring at the two walking away.

"Yes, I think this will work out well."

Clapping his hands together, he says, "Follow me and I'll show you where we have your room set up and explain a little more of what to expect while being part of our team."

Following him through a large doorway, it opens up into a hallway with multiple doors lining each side and at the end, two large double doors.

"So the first door here on the left is an equipment room. Riding gear for the boys, and any extra supplies for you as well," he starts to explain as we walk down the hallway.

He opens the door and I pop my head around the corner. It's a pretty large room and on one side is split into two, one with equipment with the number nineteen on it and the other with the number twenty-two. I become irritated with myself when I realize I'm wondering which number is Kade's. Why do I care?

On the opposite side is shelves full of medical supplies that I will need. I take a mental note to come back in here a little later to take inventory of what is here. Stepping back out into the hallway, I follow Michael to the next door.

"This is the office. My wife who runs everything should be in here." He opens the door and steps to the side to allow me to enter first.

A woman sitting at the desk looks up and smiles. "You must be Ms. Mitchell. I'm Tracy." She stands up and walks around the desk, her hand outstretched to me.

Shaking her hand, I instantly like her. How did such a cocky guy come out of these two people? "Mrs. Maddox, it is very nice to meet you."

"Please, call me Tracy."

"Only if you call me Cammie."

Her laugh is soft. "It's a deal. May I ask what Cammie is short for?"

"Camille."

"What a beautiful name for a beautiful woman."

I feel my cheeks heat up. I've never been good with taking compliments. "Thank you."

"Listen, you need anything, please don't hesitate to come and visit me. It gets a little boring in here sometimes."

I instantly love this woman. "I'm sure I will take you up on that offer. It is very nice to meet you."

Stepping out of the office, I follow Michael down to a door at the end of the hall on the left side. "This is our lunch room/meeting room."

Again, he opens the door and I just stick my head inside. A soda machine and a vending machine stand against one wall. A fridge, sink, and microwave line the back wall and a large dark table sits in the middle. I notice how clean and organized everything is. I am about to step back when I notice a wall inside lined with four very large pictures. Stepping into the room, I walk over to the wall. Above the pictures are the words "Sandy Racing." The first two pictures are of a rider, both pictures taken when the rider was up in the air. The second row I notice has one in the air and one going around a corner with dirt flying in the air. Two different riders. I can't see their faces but I can tell it's two different people.

I'm going to assume they are Kade and the other rider, Cody, I think Michael said his name was.

"Sandy Racing is the team name?" I find that I can't stop staring at the first two pictures. There is something there that's drawing me into it, I'm just not sure what. The pictures are impressive, all of them are great shots, but something about these two keep drawing me in and I'm not able to look away.

"Yes, actually named after Kade's grandmother, my wife's mom. Her name was Cassandra, they called her Sandy. Kade was her life, they even shared the same birth date, February the second."

My eyes go to the number on the plate of the motorcycle. Twenty-two, it has to be Kade in this picture. "She has passed?"

Michael nods his head. "Yes, about four months ago. She was Kade's biggest fan, she never missed a race. He did no wrong in her eyes."

"These are great pictures."

"My niece, Krystal, is a photographer and is usually at all the races, she took these. She stops in here routinely so I'm sure you will be meeting her soon. Come on, let me finish the tour up."

Turning away from the pictures, I follow Michael out of the room, looking back one last time before I step into the hallway. Why am I so drawn to this guy, even in photos? I don't like anything about this guy so far from what I've seen.

Passing one door, Michael points without stopping. "This one is Kade's room." He walks up to the next one and knocks. "This is Cody's. I'm not sure if he is here or not."

I'm surprised when a woman opens the door. "Hello, Uncle Mike."

Uncle Mike? I thought this was Cody's room.

"Krystal, this is Cammie Mitchell, our new team medic. Cammie, this is my niece and the photographer I was telling you about, Krystal. She is also dating Cody."

"Which took my uncle here forever to be all right with." Krystal hugs Michael and sends him the biggest puppy dog eyes I've ever seen.

"Still can't say I'm crazy about the idea." He wraps an arm around her in a protective fashion.

Krystal rolls her eyes up at her uncle. "Still not convincing me of that." Pulling away from her uncle she turns to me, a hand outstretched. "Hi, Cammie, it's nice to meet you."

She is very bubbly, I'm pretty sure I'm going to get along with her, no doubt about it. "It's nice to meet you, too."

A red-headed guy, looking to be in his late teens, early twenties, freckles all over his face, maybe around six feet tall, steps out of the room. "What's going on out here?"

"Cammie, this is Cody, our two-fifty rider. Cody, this is our new team medic, Cammie." Michael makes the introduction.

"Welcome to the team, Cammie," Cody extends his hand to me.

"Thank you, so far I'm thinking this is going to be a great team to work with." *Well, maybe with the exception of the team's other rider*, I think to myself.

"Come on, Cammie, let me show you to your office. Cody, why don't you meet me on the track in fifteen, Kade is already out there."

"Sure, no problem. Cammie, nice meeting you." Cody disappears back into the room, Krystal waves as she follows him inside and closes the door.

"Come on, your office is right down here." Michael walks down to the end of the hall where the double doors are.

Opening one door, he steps aside to allow me to enter first. I freeze at the first glimpse of the area. There is no way this is my office. I was expecting to walk into a small room with maybe a massage/exam table in the middle, possibly a shelf on one wall with some of the supplies I would need, not this state-of-the-art, fully loaded gym.

This is something I would expect a major league sports team to have for their players, not a small, two-person racing team. There are two matching tables that can be used for either massages or exams. A full weight system is in one corner, a whirlpool tub and another for ice therapy, along with a large ice-making machine against one wall. Along another long wall is just cabinets and I can only imagine what supplies are in there, and then I remember the first room that had overflow. These guys aren't leaving anything to spare, they want to make sure they are ready for just about anything. Looking to my right I notice another door, walking over I enter to find a small office.

"You can decorate it any way you feel comfortable." Michael's voice comes from behind me.

"This is all incredible. I will admit I'm a little surprised by how equipped you are here for a two-person team."

"Believe it or not, a year ago we were working out of a couple of motorhomes and trailers. We started the build about then, just finished it up right before Sandy passed away. My mother-in-law wanted the best, she paid to have this place built. Only the best for her boy she would always say. She'd tell us she couldn't take the money with her and she didn't want the family fighting over it, and she always wanted to make sure Kade was taken care of. He was her only grandchild." I hear the pride in his voice as he looks around the office, but there is sadness as well. The family sounds like they are all pretty close. "Well, I'm going to leave you to look around, check things out, make sure there isn't anything you need that we may have forgotten. Just make a list and I'll get it from you later today."

A list, I can't image they have missed a thing. I just nod, still a little shocked. I hear the door shut behind me. Taking a deep breath, I look around my office. I round the large dark desk and sit down in the office chair. Sitting on the desk is a computer, I have a filing cabinet against one wall and two chairs on the other side of my desk. There is a large plant in the corner but other than that nothing else. The only thing decorating the walls is above the door, a metal cutout that reads 'Sandy Racing.'

Pulling my phone out of my pocket, I swipe the screen to open it up, find Lucas's number and wait while it rings. Like before, it goes to voicemail. "I'm starting to think you are hiding from me. Give me a call later."

CHAPTER TWO

KADE

"Kade, what's going on with you today? Your times are all over the place and nowhere near what they need to be."

My dad is right and I can feel how off I am with every run. What the hell is my problem today? "Maybe I should run the outside track." What I think that'll change I have no idea, but I needed to come up with some excuse.

"Are you hurting?" Dad walks over to me, pointing at my knee.

I shrug, I could use that as an excuse, he would believe me, but it's not my knee. "Look, we can't risk it. Why don't you go and see Cammie, have her work a little on it. It's nice to have her here now, I feel a little better knowing she can work that knee on a regular basis."

My knee isn't bothering me, but at the mention of Cammie's name I'm thinking it may be a little tight. Earlier today, I saw the way she gave me a once over when we met. She liked what she saw, her dark blue eyes darkened up even more, almost giving them the effect of being a midnight blue. Her cheeks turned red, she shifted from foot to foot and her hands were fidgety. I also didn't miss the moment she noticed Brooke standing next to me, she instantly became irritated and short with a disgusted look on her face.

"Kade, maybe we should call it a day, you seem distracted." Dad grabs the front bar of my bike, his head motioning toward the exit, "Go on, I'll get Kyle to put your bike up." He nods his head to the guy who joined us a couple of months ago.

Kyle is a great guy, just had some bad luck. That guy would have made a name for himself in the racing world if it hadn't been for his accident he had two years ago. Broke his back during a race and it almost paralyzed him. It reminds a rider what can happen out there on the track, but he is a great team member.

Pulling my helmet off, I hang it from my handle bar, then kick my leg over the seat and leave my bike to my dad. Cody makes a lap past us. "He is looking good, he will take the two-fifty this year for sure if he keeps riding like that."

Dad nods, watching Cody. "He's a good rider and he isn't cocky, which makes him a great rider."

"Are you saying I'm cocky, Dad?"

Dad laughs and nods his head. "Not you, Kade, not at all. You aren't rude about it, but you know you're good which is what scares me a little. You have no fear and you don't know when to slow down."

"That's what you are here for, to slow me down," I pat him on the shoulder.

"Well, I'm slowing you down now. You're off today, call it a day. Go see Cammie, have her work that knee and we will get back to it tomorrow."

"Yes, sir." Walking away, I see Brooke walking toward me. I thought she had left, she was pissed I wouldn't let her watch me practice today.

"You done for the day, babe?" Her smile is telling me she is hoping so and that I'm going to make a little time for her now.

Usually I'd be more than happy to "make a little time for her" but right now I'm not in the mood.

"I'm on my way to get my knee worked out and not sure how long it will take. I'll call you later and maybe we can meet up then."

Her lip goes into a pout and I have to stop myself from rolling my eyes. "You promise to call me later?" Walking up to me, she wraps her hand around the back of my head and pulls my lips down to hers. Her body rubs up against mine, but strangely it isn't affecting me at all.

"Kade, get over and see Cammie about that knee now!" Dad yells from the other side of the track.

Brooke pulls away and sends a glare over in my dad's direction. No wonder my dad doesn't like her. He gives me that look, I know what he means. I almost want to thank him. Brooke gives me one last kiss on the lips and then turns and walks away. I watch her for a moment, relieved she is leaving. Looking back at my dad, I wave at him and then make my way to our new trainer.

Pushing through one of the doors to the training center, I notice it's empty. The door to the office is open, walking over I poke my head inside and find no one. Cammie isn't in here. I'll go and grab a shower real fast and maybe she will be back by then.

Turning, I head for the door. Pulling it open, I find myself chest to face with the feisty brunette. Cammie's face is directly in my chest, my arms are braced on each side of the door trying to keep from falling back. Moments ago when Brooke was plastered against me, rubbing all up on me, I had no reaction at all. Right now my body is on fire and I have to fight the need to wrap my arms around the body pressed against me.

Cammie quickly regains herself, stepping away from me. I have to fight the urge to reach out and pull her against me again.

"I'm so sorry, I didn't realize anyone was in here." She stammers around, not even looking up at me.

"It's my fault."

Her eyes shoot up at me in surprise. "Is there something you needed?"

"Actually, yes, I was hoping you could work my knee out a little."

"What's wrong with it?"

Right now nothing, but if it gets her hands on me then it hurts. "Old injury, it just flared up during practice today."

"If you will let me inside then we can go and have a look." She looks around me into the room, waiting for me to move aside to allow her to enter. "I mean I could try and check it out here in the hallway, but it would definitely be easier in there," she points around me.

"I'm actually going to go grab a shower real fast, if you don't mind?" Moving aside, I wait for her to enter the room and then I step out.

"Not a problem, I'll see you in a few." She doesn't even turn around, she just disappears into the office, leaving me standing in the hallway.

I'm shocked! I'm sure it puts me in the conceited department for thinking this, but women don't usually ignore me like Cammie just did. I'm not sure if it impresses me about her or insults me. Now that I think about it, she never even really looked at me the whole time we were talking. Thinking back to earlier today when we met, I know I didn't imagine the look she was giving me.

Why am I obsessing about this? Sure, she is beautiful, but there are lots of beautiful woman out there. Entering my room, I pull my shirt up over my head and throw it onto one of the chairs. Entering the bathroom, I quickly strip out of the rest of my gear and turn on the shower water.

My grandmother spared no expense when it came to this training center. Cody and I each have our own room with a full bathroom, small kitchenette and living room setup. I wasn't expecting anywhere near the magnitude of this place when she announced that she would be building the team a training facility. We are probably better equipped than most of the large teams in this sport.

After a quick shower I grab a pair of basketball style shorts and a t-shirt. If Cammie is going to work on my knee this is the easiest thing to wear. Glancing over, I spot the picture on the table next to the couch of my grandmother and me. My heart tugs and tears burn the backs of my eyes. She has been gone for about four months now and I still find myself waiting for her to barge in through the door like she always did. Sitting down on the couch, I grab the picture. I know she spoiled me. I was her world, her only grandchild, and she had enough money to probably buy the state of Texas if she really wanted to.

She was also my biggest fan. She never missed a race and was always there to be the first one to hug me at the finish line. Everyone knew to stay out of her way, she was always the first one to congratulate me. There are not words to express how much I miss her, being on the track and finishing a race knowing she isn't going to be there is hard.

A heavy knock on my door has me wiping my eyes and putting the picture back on the table. The door opens and my dad pops his head in. I see the question in his eyes but he looks over onto the table and finds his answer.

"I thought you would be over with Cammie getting that knee rolled out."

"I'm on my way, wanted to grab a shower real fast." Getting up from the couch, I walk over to leave my room.

"You good?" There is still some concern in his eyes.

"It's been a long day is all. I'm going to have my knee rolled out and then head home." Honestly, I'd like to skip the knee part and go straight home, but I know my dad is concerned.

Shutting the door behind me, my dad puts a hand on my

shoulder. "Get some rest. We have a race this weekend and we need to make sure you are ready. Tomorrow I'm thinking we need to work on the outside terrain with both of you."

"Sounds good." Heading over to the training room, I wave to my dad as I walk away. I want to get this done so I can go home.

Walking in, I'm greeted by Cammie standing on a chair stretching to reach something on a top shelf of one of the cabinets. Her shirt is raised just slightly and a small amount of her skin from her back is showing. My hands tingle with a need to reach out and touch that small section of skin.

"Maybe I should tell my dad you need a foot stool."

Cammie jumps at the sound of my voice and the chair wobbles under her. I hear her curse under her breath but can't make out what she says. I launch forward to try and stop her from falling off the chair, but she manages to rebalance herself before the chair can tip over.

Her hands grasping the doors of the cabinet, her head is bent forward and she takes a couple deep breaths. The small of her back is still exposed, I can't help myself from touching her. Even though she is steady on the chair, I place my hand at the small of her back.

"Sorry, didn't mean to scare you." Her back stiffens at my touch. I almost pull my hand away because of the heat that radiates through my skin, but it's intoxicating and I can't seem to move.

She nods her head and steps down from the chair. I have no choice but to remove my hand now and I find myself disappointed that I no longer feel the warmth I did just moments ago. What the hell is wrong with me?

She never looks at me, she just moves away and stands next to the table. "Go ahead and have a seat, tell me what you did to your knee."

Walking over, I sit up on the table and watch as she grabs a notebook from the counter and sits on a nearby stool.

"The beginning of last year I fractured my patella in my knee and ruptured ligaments. I'm lucky that we didn't need to take the surgery route, but after a day of practicing it's sore so I usually take a couple days a week and go and have it worked on in physical therapy. Dad is liking the idea that we have you now and we can work on it a little more regularly."

As I speak she is busy writing everything down, never once does she look up from the notebook on her lap.

"All right, so those injuries can be a bothersome for the rest of your life, especially with the amount of strain you put on it with the jumping you do. We can start a routine treatment that will hopefully help with the pain and discomfort, but that knee will probably always give you problems."

I like this one, she doesn't sugar coat anything. "I figured, but a little relief is better than none and that's all I need right now, something to take the edge off I guess you can say. I'm not ready to give up riding, and why would I give it up when it's going to bother me if I'm riding or not? If I'm going to suffer through some pain I'm going to be doing what I love while I can."

She still hasn't looked up from that damn notebook, she just sits there nodding her head as I talk. Stretching my neck, I try to look over and catch what she is writing down but I can't see anything with the angle she has the notebook. The silence in the room is a little more than I can take. "So what are you thinking?"

She lays the book onto her lap, face down. Now I am really curious about what she was writing down. She takes a deep breath and finally looks up at me. Take that back, she looks up, but she looks everywhere other than directly at me.

"I'm thinking we can rotate a routine between cold therapy, workouts and massaging. I can't say it will fix it but it should keep it from getting any worse. With the intense pressure you put on it from riding, I'm just going to try and keep it from getting worse."

Quickly standing up, she heads for the office and I watch

through the window as she sets the notebook down on the desk. She places her hands on the desk and looks around like she is searching for something, I personally think she is stalling.

"Cammie, do you have a problem with me or something?" I ask loud enough for her to hear me in the office.

CHAPTER THREE

Now that's a loaded question! When he placed his hand on my back earlier I had to fight the need turn around and jump into his arms, beg him to touch me all over. I wanted to feel that tingling feeling throughout my whole body, not just that small area of my back. I haven't been able to look him in the eye since. I'm too afraid that he will see right through me. I'm still trying to figure it out myself. My body may be reacting to his touch but my head is saying something completely different. I don't want to be attracted to him in any way, body or mind. From what I saw attached to his arm when we met earlier today, I shouldn't want anything to do with him. He wants a play toy and I don't fall in that category, no matter how good-looking the guy is. It kind of pisses me off that I've had a reaction to anything this man may do.

He was cocky this morning, one of those guys who knows he is good at what he does, maybe even the best, but not humble at all. He knows he can have the girl, all he has to do is smile her way and she would fall into his arms, shedding her clothes on her walk over to him.

I have to admit, tonight something is different. He isn't

wearing his cocky grin and his eyes look shaded I guess you can say, almost sad.

I've asked all the questions I can and I need to snap out of this and be professional. I needed to step away for a moment. My office seemed like a good place to collect my thoughts. Am I having a problem with him? *Yes!* I want to yell.

Shake it off, Cammie, you've had a lot happen today, nerves running high on a new job and getting settled in. Go in there and do your damn job! I scold myself.

Taking a deep breath, I walk back into the room, this time making sure to make eye contact. "Sorry, it's been an eventful day is all. I have no reason to have an issue with you, I'm sorry I gave that impression. Go ahead and bring your legs over the side of the table, we will start with some stretches and then roll it out a little today. Tomorrow I'd like you to sit in the ice bath before you go out and practice. We will start out there and then put a routine together that will work best as we go for the next couple days, figure out what helps and what doesn't."

Throwing his legs over the edge, he just nods his head. It's like a whole different person. No smart-ass remarks, no smirking, nothing. He almost looks defeated. I don't know him well enough to ask if everything is all right. I don't think personal questions are appropriate yet. I need to stay professional which means do the work I'm hired to do and that's all.

Grabbing some oil off the shelf behind me, I rub it in between my hands. I take a deep breath, not sure if I'm nervous because this is the first time I've actually worked outside of school, although I've done a ton of this during school so what would be so different now? Or, is it the man I'm about to work on?

Pull yourself together, Cammie, you can't lose your job over a guy, especially one who thinks women are only made to fill the bed at night. Turning back to Kade, I place a hand on each side of his knee. Kade jumps, scaring the crap out of me causing me to take a step back, my oil-covered hands flying up in a surrender position in the air.

"Did I hurt you? I'm sorry," I ramble off quickly. His leg shouldn't hurt that bad this far out from an original injury. If it does we have to take a different approach completely, starting with getting him off the motorcycle.

Kade's knuckles are white as both hands grasp the side of the table, his head hanging down to his chest. I see his jaw flex and I have to stop a moan from escaping. There is something that happens every time I see a guy flex his jaw. I know it makes me a little on the strange side. It's a control action I always say. Even if a guy is mad, upset, turned on, it's a control action. Them trying to hold themselves back, restraint. My best friend in college, Sam, would always tease me about it but I can't help but find it completely sexy.

His head comes up and our eyes meet. There is no pain or anger in them, they don't look sad or clouded. The green has changed to a jade color. His jaw flexes once again. The definition in his jaw makes my hands ache to reach up and touch him. This time I can't hold back the moan that escapes from my throat.

"Don't make that sound, Cammie. I'm having a hard enough time keeping my hands to myself."

I should be shocked, maybe even mad, but instead I'm finding it hard to keep my distance and find myself closing the gap between us. Pushing myself in between his legs, my stomach is now pressed against the edge of the table, his hands still in a death grip on the edge of the table. I shouldn't be doing this, my career may end before it even gets started if I don't back myself up, but I'm pretty confident it's already too late.

Before I can really think too hard about the consequences my arm loops around his neck, keeping in mind that my hands are covered in oil. My core starts to hum and I realize I'm about to make the biggest mistake, but I have no ability or desire to stop myself.

Bringing my lips down to his, my other hand goes to his jaw. I feel the flex under my palm and I have to control myself from climbing up onto his lap. His lips are soft, his tongue is demanding. His fingers are now buried in my hair, deepening the kiss, his chest pressed tight against mine. I can feel the vibration run through him as a deep moan escapes from him.

As quickly as this all starts, it ends just as fast when his hands drop to my shoulders and he pushes me away, so hard that I stumble back a couple of steps and have to catch my balance before I end up on the floor.

What the hell just happened? What was I thinking? The obvious answer to that is I wasn't thinking. He was right to push me away. "Kade, I'm sorry. I have no idea..."

I'm not given the chance to finish, Kade quickly jumps off the table and heads for the door. Without a word from him, the door slams behind him.

I can't move, my feet are stuck to the floor. I should be running after him asking him to forgive me, to not fire me. My lips are throbbing from our kiss, so much so that I have to believe he wanted that kiss as much as I did, but that is no excuse, it shouldn't have happened. My hands are shaking, what have I done? I'm offered the chance at an amazing job and I go and screw it up because I couldn't control myself with my boss's son.

Earlier I looked down at a woman who I felt was only hanging onto Kade for image and sex and here I throw myself at him basically the same way. Worst part is he pushed me away and walked away from me, what's that say about me?

Plopping down onto my nearby stool because I'm pretty sure my legs are going to give out, I lean forward, my elbows on my knees, and bury my face in my hands. I'm waiting to feel anger, at myself of course, but all I feel is a need, one that pulses in my core just thinking about how his lips felt against mine or the way I felt like he was possessing me with his hands digging into my hair and holding me tight against him.

I have never kissed nor been kissed by a guy like that before and even though I'm pretty sure I'm going to be fired, the only thing I can think about is the need to kiss him again. Maybe I just need to grab my stuff and quit before I can be fired. Problem is I'm sure Kade went straight to his father and demanded that I be let go.

I'm not going to wait around. I won't be able to face either of them if they come in here right now, the embarrassment would be more than I can handle. If I leave now they would have to call, I can even let it go to voicemail and not have to talk to them at all.

Grow up, Cammie, you did this, you need to stand up and face the repercussions in person. Walking into my office, I gather my stuff and then sit down at the desk and wait for Michael.

Looking around as I wait, this is where the anger starts to bubble up. This office is pretty bare and I had plans today after work to go and buy some stuff to bring a little life into it. I have an office, a great job, and I screw it up completely. Why Kade? It's not like I haven't worked on good-looking guys before. Athletes that were drop-dead gorgeous and built, but never have I been unable to control myself around one of them. What's so different with Kade? Why did I throw myself at him?

The door to the training room opens and Michael enters. Here we go! Taking a deep breath, I stand and meet him in the training room.

"I hear you need a stool."

Wait, what? "A stool?"

"Yes, Kade just came to my office and said we needed to get you a stool. He said he came in and found you trying to reach for something on a chair and almost fell off. We can't have you getting hurt. I'll make sure you have one tomorrow. Is there anything else you need?"

Kade had gone to his office and all he said was I needed a stool? I'm so confused right now. I'm waiting for the bomb to drop and Michael to start yelling or some kind of words of disappointment to be thrown at me.

"Cammie, is everything okay?"

"Umm, sorry. Yes, I'm fine," I lie completely. There are so many reasons right now why I am not all right.

"So is there anything else that you need?"

Yes, for him to explain to me how I still have my job after I attacked his son. Why didn't Kade say anything to his dad? "No, sir, there is nothing I need, thank you. You have stocked everything that I may need from what I can see."

"All right, good. Well, I hope you have a great evening, we will see you tomorrow." He turns and walks out, just like that.

Staring at the door, I wait. He is going to come back through that door at any moment and tell me how stupid I am for thinking I was going to get away with any of this. But after what feels like an hour of standing here, no one walks through the doors.

Turning back to the office, I grab my stuff off the desk and walk back to the door. Opening it slowly, I'm expecting to see one of them standing there, disappointment in their eyes, asking me not to come back tomorrow, but again to my surprise, no one is in the hallway.

Quickly I walk down the hall, out of the practice arena and out to my car. Plopping down into my seat, I shut the door and take a deep breath, my head falls back against my headrest and I close my eyes. What a day. How do I still have a job?

My phone ringing causes me to jump in my seat, hitting my knees on the steering wheel. Would they have waited until I was out before telling me they didn't want me back? Hesitantly, I pick my phone up and turn it over. Lucas's face is on the screen, his name written across it.

Taking a deep breath, I stare at the phone in disbelief. Swiping the screen, I answer. "Hi."

"Well that didn't sound good. Not a good first day?"

"Why didn't you answer my calls this morning? Why did you lead me to believe this was a job for a bull rider, not a motocross rider?" As my questions are pouring out of my mouth, I hear him laughing on the other end of the line. If I could reach out and slap him, I would.

"Cammie, calm down! Was it that bad?"

Was it that bad? I kissed my boss's son today! I wanted to yell through the phone. "The easiest way to explain my day is a day full of surprises. Why didn't you tell me who I was going to be working for?"

"Why didn't you ask more questions before you started and Michael was emailing you?" he throws back to me. "Does it really matter if Kade is a bull rider or a motorcycle rider? Michael needed someone to join the team and I thought of you. He was interested, you were excited, and it all seemed to work out."

He's right, I should have done a little more research on this job. Assuming isn't a way to start a new job. It's just proof that I have messed up in more ways than one where this job is concerned. "I'm sorry, I should just be saying thank you for helping me get in here. It's just the stress of a 'first day on the job' kind of thing. Michael is really nice. This place is impressive. I even have an office."

"Wow, not bad for a first job right out of school. Have you met Kade yet?"

Like he knew we were talking about him, Kade walks out of the training center. My skin tingles and my lips start to throb, the same way they felt right after we kissed. I watch as he walks across the parking lot and to a lifted black Chevy truck. He climbs up into the cab and I watch while he rests his head back against the seat for a moment. His truck is facing my car. The parking lot isn't big so I can see him clearly through his front windshield. He rubs his hands over his face and at the moment he brings his head away from the seat rest, his eyes lock with mine. I can't read his expression and I can't look away. After what seems like forever, though I'm sure is only moments, he slowly shakes his head, almost like he is telling me no and then breaks eye contact with me. Quickly he starts up his truck and peels out of the parking spot.

"Cammie, are you still there?" Lucas's voice breaks through my foggy mind.

"Sorry! I'm going to talk to you later, I just want to go home and soak in a tub. Start fresh tomorrow."

"Wow, well you don't seem to want to tell me many details so call me later if you want to talk, maybe we can meet up for dinner soon."

I start up my car. "Sounds good. Hey, Lucas, thank you for helping me get this job. I do appreciate it."

"I knew you would be great for them. Call me later." He hangs up before I can say anything else.

I'M NOT sure how I end up at home, sitting in the driveway, or how long I've been sitting here, but it must have been a while because my dad scares the crap out of me when he knocks on my driver's side window.

Putting up a finger to tell him to give me a second, I go to turn off my car and realize I already did it, but not sure when. Grabbing my stuff off the passenger seat, I open my door and step out.

"Honey, are you all right? Your mom says you have been sitting here for a while. Thought maybe you were on the phone but when I got out here you were just staring."

"Sorry, Dad, I'm good. I was just thinking of things I wanted to get for my new office." I force a smile for my dad. There is no way I can tell him I may not have a job tomorrow because I couldn't get myself under control around my boss's son.

My dad walks next to me as we head to the front door. "You have your own office?" Opening the front door, he steps aside and allows me to enter first. "Your mom is in the kitchen."

I want to make some excuse about being exhausted from my first day on a new job, but I know my parents are excited for me and will have lots of questions. Kade had plenty of time to tell his dad to let me go and he didn't, maybe everything will be all right.

"Cammie, is everything all right? You were sitting out in your car for some time. Was everything what you thought it would be, meet any cute bull riders?" Mom shoots out the questions the moment I set foot in the kitchen.

The kitchen smells great and I'm reminded I haven't eaten anything today. I was so nervous this morning and I was so busy checking everything out in the training room and my office that by the time I thought about lunch it was already after three and I figured I might as well wait. I knew Mom would be cooking dinner, and in this house it is always around six.

Sitting down on a bar stool, I drop my purse onto the counter. "Well, that was one of the largest surprises of the day. I'm not working with any bull riders." Mom looks over her shoulder at me from the stove, confusion etched on her face. "I'm actually working for a motocross race team."

"You mean like dirt bikes?" Dad props his hip against the counter next to me.

"Yep!" I confirm, nodding my head.

"Do you know anything about that sport at all?" Mom places a lid on the pan and turns to me.

"Not a thing, but an injury is an injury. So doing my job isn't going to be affected by the fact that I have absolutely no knowledge of the sport. Don't get me wrong, I'm going to do a little homework tonight about it so I don't sound like a complete idiot when I'm around the team, but you guys should see the setup they have there, it's huge."

"How many riders are you working with?" Dad raises an eyebrow in question.

"Only two, but this training center is built for a huge team. Michael, the owner, explained that his mother-in-law had lots of money and his son Kade, one of the riders, was her only grandson. Long story short, he walked on water in her eyes, she wanted the best for him, so she built him this training center and it's huge. My room is stocked out for a professional football team, I have everything and then some, plus an office."

"Sounds exciting. Have you met any of the riders?" Mom smiles over at me. Does she know? She has always been able to read me, I couldn't hide anything from her growing up.

Looking down, I play with the strap of my purse. Maybe if I don't look at her... "Yes, I met both of them today. Kade and Cody."

"How are they?" Mom keeps pushing.

I just shrug my shoulders, but I can feel my cheeks heating up. *I can say Kade is one hell of a kisser*, I think to myself. "They are all right, I guess. Just a quick meet today, I'm sure tomorrow will be more involved. Today I just became familiar with everything."

Looking up at my mom, she is giving me that look. Damn it, she knows I'm hiding something. "I'm going to go clean up a little, dinner smells like it's almost finished and I'm starving." Getting up, I grab my purse and leave the kitchen before Mom can ask any more questions. Although I'm sure dinner conversation is going to be based around today, but I need to collect myself a little before.

CHAPTER FOUR

KADE

Again, my phone lights up next to me. It's Brooke, I don't even have to look over to know. On the way home I ran through a drive-thru, grabbing a burger for dinner and all I want to do right now is eat, enjoy my one beer I'm allowing myself for the night and relax.

I'm exhausted and I have no idea why. Sure, I ran some laps today, but I didn't ride hard, hell, none of my lap times came even close to my usual. I didn't go out last night and I actually got a good night of sleep, but my mind hasn't stopped today. Well, at least not since I met our new team medic.

Lucas had told us he had the perfect person for us to hire when my dad mentioned we were looking for someone. I never paid too much attention when they talked about it. Once Lucas told us this was a good friend from school I kind of assumed we were hiring some guy. How wrong I found myself to be today when I was introduced to Cammie.

There she stood, jeans, button-up white shirt and cowboy boots. So simple of a look, but it caught my attention right away. I watched as she checked me out. I know it makes me sound arrogant but I know I'm not hard to look at. I saw the change in her eyes as she appreciated what she saw, that is until her eyes landed on Brooke standing next to me. Her reaction completely changed and she became cold toward me. I know what Cammie was thinking about Brooke and I get it. She was dressed to barely cover anything on her body, high heels, which doesn't make sense when we are on a dirt track, and she is very clingy, but we have had a few good conversations when she doesn't seem so "airy" I guess would be a good word to use to describe her. Sure, she isn't someone I would look at having the happy married life with, but I'm not looking for that right now anyway, I'm completely dedicated to racing and becoming number one. Brooke is someone fun to hang around with. Normally all is good, but since meeting Cammie this morning and my dad telling her she had to leave, she has been calling non-stop.

My mind hasn't shut down since that kiss with Cammie earlier. I've never pushed a girl away before, or ran out like a scared school boy who just kissed his first girl. Something about that kiss was like no other, though. I've kissed my share of women, but even from the moment Cammie's fingers touched the back of my neck I felt an electrical shock shoot through my body. I've never had a reaction like that to a woman, I'll admit it kind of freaked me out.

I can only imagine what she is thinking, in the parking lot when I was leaving I would swear she almost had a worried look on her face when she looked up and our eyes met before I pulled out of the parking spot. More like peeled out of the parking lot. I can only imagine what she is thinking.

Now that I think back to our time in her room, I'm not even sure what happened. One minute she was acting like she would rather be anywhere than there and the next she released the sexiest moan I think I've ever heard and then we were kissing. Not a small kiss on the lips either. It was the nails digging in the back of my scalp, body instantly becoming hot, tongues meeting kind of kiss. I think what shocked me to the point where I had to push her away was even as hot as the kiss was, all I wanted to do was pull her in close and keep her safe. I became protective, or maybe possessive might be a better word. I didn't want to let her go and that's what caused me to push her away, as strange as that sounds. I have never been affected that way.

Again, my phone vibrates next to me. Damn, she isn't giving up and I'm guessing if I don't answer it she isn't going to quit. Without looking at the phone, I grab it and push the green button. "Brooke, not tonight."

"Well now I'm just disappointed, big guy, and here I was hoping for so much more." A male's voice comes through the phone.

"Lucas?" I pull the phone away and verify by looking at the picture on my screen, that's Lucas all right.

"Wow, telling Brooke no, rough day?" He's laughing through the phone.

"Sorry, man. Just wanting to relax tonight is all and she hasn't stopped calling, I thought you were her again."

"Rough day at the center?"

Rough day? Not sure I'd say rough, but definitely eventful, I think to myself. "No, just been a little off day is all. I decided to just relax tonight, even my times were off."

I met Lucas three years ago. One of my friends that used to help out on race days brought him along to a race. Lucas got hooked and we have been good friends since.

"So what did you think about Cammie?"

"Man, you could have mentioned your good friend was a girl."

"Would it have made a difference? Your dad knew she was a woman, why is this something you didn't know? Maybe you should be a little more involved in what is going on there at the center instead of just riding around the track and playing with women."

"I'm involved with the important stuff, man. I guess I just assumed when you said you had a good friend from school that would be perfect for the job, you were talking about a guy is all. It was just a surprise." I wanted to ask how Cammie and he could only be friends, a man would have to be swinging for the same side if he wasn't attracted to Cammie, but I knew that would bring up questions from him I just didn't want to get into right now.

Lucas starts laughing on the other end. "What's so funny?"

"Well, this is kind of the same conversation I had with Cammie today. Let's just say she wasn't expecting to be working with someone who rides motorcycles for a living."

"Who did she think she was working for?"

"If you didn't notice, Cammie is all about country. She assumed you were a bull rider. I believe she was a little confused this morning when she pulled up and saw not a bull in sight. Well, with all of the surprises to the side, everything work out all right today?"

I wonder what his response would be if I told him I kissed his good friend today on her first day of work. "Everything went fine, really didn't spend much time with her today."

There, that wasn't a lie. I only spent maybe at the most twenty minutes all day around her.

"I promise you guys won't be disappointed with her, she is great. Well, man, I'll try to stop by soon, don't forget I need the dates for the races. If you guys want me tagging along to help out, I need to mark off at work. Sorry I can't be there this weekend to help out."

Lucas had started hanging out at the races so much that he picked up on all the mechanics of the bikes pretty fast. He's ended up traveling with us most of the time to help out.

"Sorry, that keeps slipping my mind. Text me tomorrow and remind me and I'll have Mom email it over to you."

"Sounds good, talk to you later."

"Later." Hanging up, I go to put the phone down on the table when it starts to vibrate again. The screen lights up and Brooke's face appears. She just isn't getting the hint right now. I swipe the phone to ignore and turn the sound all the way down. I'm done for the night.

PULLING INTO THE CENTER, I spot Cammie's car right away. I can hear Cody out and running already when I jump down from my truck. I'm late and I know my dad isn't going to be happy about it.

Walking into the center, Mom is walking out of her office. "Hey, Mom, can you email the updated schedule over to Lucas? He was asking for it, I know we have made some changes."

"Sure but you need to go and get out there. Your father is already fuming that you are late this morning."

"I know, I turned my phone down last night and didn't hear the alarm this morning."

"Well you better hurry and get out there." She starts to walk past me. "Oh, I almost forgot, Cammie was looking for you this morning. You may want to stop by her office before you go out."

Really, Cammie was looking for me this morning? I try to hide the surprise but I see the questioning look my mom is giving me. "We started a treatment for my knee yesterday, she's probably just checking up on if I'm swinging by today."

"Has your knee been bothering you?" She looks down at my leg, concern etched across her forehead.

"Mom, I'm fine. Dad just wants me to start working it regularly now that Cammie is here, make sure it's all good for the races. It's been fine, really haven't had any pain at all."

She searches my face, trying to decide if I'm telling her the truth. After getting hurt she tried to get me to take this season off as well. I'm sure it's a "mom thing" but I assured her I was fine and needed to get back to the track.

"All right, well go see Cammie and then get out to the track before your father comes looking for you again." She smiles and heads down the hall.

When she disappears through the doors, I turn and head over to the training room. Pushing open the door, Cammie is not inside. Looking over at her office, I see her sitting at her desk. Taking a deep breath, I can't figure out why all of a sudden I'm nervous. I don't get nervous around women so what the hell is my problem right now? So we kissed, not like I haven't kissed women before.

Walking over, I knock on the door frame. "My mom said you were looking for me."

She looks up from her computer and something jumps in my chest. What the hell is that all about?

CHAPTER FIVE

CAMMIE

This morning I woke up and decided that I needed to start acting like a professional, starting with coming to work and apologizing to Kade for what happened yesterday. Now that he is standing here in my office, I can't seem to do anything other than stare at him like an idiot. Maybe I should just throw up my hands now and quit, this is insane. Why the heck is this guy affecting me like this?

"My mom said you were looking for me. What's up?"

So casual, like nothing happened between us yesterday. Maybe I'm making too much out of this. Come on, I saw the girl he was with, it's not like kissing me would be any different than the tons of women he has probably kissed. He did however push me away, maybe I should just let it go and move forward like he seems to be doing. I might be saving myself some embarrassment if I don't bring it back up. I'm pretty sure I don't want to hear that I'm a terrible kisser, or I repulsed him or something.

No, I'm a professional and I want to make sure he takes me serious as one. Getting up from my chair, I round my desk and lean against it for some support. He doesn't move from the doorway.

"Um, yes, I wanted to apologize for my very unprofessional manner yesterday when I was treating you. I want to say thank you for not having me fired because of it and I want to promise you that nothing like that will happen again. I have no good excuse to what I was thinking, but I can assure you from here on out I will be doing my job with the professionalism that I didn't show yesterday."

I swear my heart is going to beat out of my chest with how nervous I am at this moment. This has to be one of the most humiliating things I have ever had to do, but what I deserve after my actions. It is taking everything in me to keep eye contact with Kade, especially now when all he is doing is staring back at me.

Nothing, he is saying nothing and I can't read what may be going through his mind at all. I would love nothing more than to crawl under this desk that I have a death grip on and hide for the remaining part of the day. How is this going to work if there is going to be so much awkwardness between us? Maybe this is just weird for me, it doesn't seem to be bothering him one bit.

Pushing away from the door, he shakes his head, laughing at me, I think.

"Cammie, don't sweat it. I'm used to girls throwing themselves at me." He shrugs his shoulders like it's no big deal.

I know my mouth must be on the floor from shock. What the heck have I been worried about? Kade is an arrogant ass. Pulling myself together, I stand on my own away from the desk and square my shoulders. "All the same, I just wanted to clear the air." Turning my back to him, I round my desk back to my chair. Sitting down, I turn my attention back to my computer and the blank screen, which he can't see, and hope he gets the hint that I'm done talking to him now and he will leave.

After a minute or so of him just standing there, I finally raise my eyes back to him in a questioning manner. He looks as though he wants to say something and I'm about to ask him what, when he finally turns and heads out of the training room.

The door closes and I slump back into my chair. Here all night I've been worried about my job, and if his father is going to fire me, when all this time he hasn't even given it a second thought. If I am being honest with myself I'm a little hurt. I felt something yesterday when we kissed, something I have never felt when I have kissed any other guy. I can't say I hoped he had felt it as well because that would be like admitting that I wouldn't mind doing it again. I think what really ticks me off is how hurt I am that he compared me to all the other girls. *Enough is enough, Cammie,* I scold myself. This morning I had decided to apologize and move past this and that's what I need to do, just look at Kade as a patient and do my job.

The door to the training center opens up again and my heart stops. Is he coming back in? No, it's Krystal and I have to remind myself to breath. I watch as she comes in and sits down in one of the chairs across from me.

"Hey, how are things going?"

I force what I hope looks like a real smile. "Good, just trying to get everything settled."

She watches me for a moment. "What's wrong?"

Well, so much for a real smile I was hoping I put on. "Nothing at all, just a little overwhelmed. I wasn't really expecting all of this when I took the job, just a lot to take in and learn is all."

"Oh, well do you need help with anything?"

Shaking my head, I take a couple deep breaths. I need to let all of this go and do what I've been hired to do. "I'm good, I think I'm getting it all. So you take all the pictures I've seen hanging in the rooms?" I change up the subject.

"That I do."

"Well you are amazing at it. The pictures I've seen are great, how long have you been doing photography?"

"High school I would say is when I really got into it. I was on the yearbook committee and decided to do sports pictures and fell in love with it. It's not my day job but it's a great hobby. During the races I take pictures of all the riders and make a little extra cash from it, but mainly I shoot for our team."

"What's your day job then?" I'm a little surprised she has a different job since she has been here both the days I have.

"I'm a vet tech at the twenty-four-hour clinic right down the street." She looks down at her watch. "Which reminds me, I need to head out. Just wanted to check on you, see if you needed anything. Get to know each other a little more, you know, that kind of stuff."

Krystal reminds me a little of my best friend from college, Sam. "Well thank you for checking up on me, I'd love to get to know each other more when you have a day off, or maybe lunch or something."

"Sure, that sounds like fun." She hands me her phone, "Here, put your number in, we will make plans. You all ready for this weekend's road trip?"

Looking over at her, I'm a little confused. "What's going on this weekend?"

"Haven't they told you? We have a race out in Vegas, we are driving up there so we are leaving on Thursday to give us enough time before the races begin."

Holy crap, this Thursday?! Tracy told me she emailed me the schedule this morning but she never mentioned having anything going on this weekend and I haven't had a chance to look at it yet. Definitely something I am going to have to do soon. "Wow, Vegas, well I guess I'm ready."

"We have so much fun on race weekends and being in Vegas is just the cherry on top."

I can't help but laugh at Krystal's enthusiasm, she makes everything sound exciting and fun. I find myself looking forward to this weekend. This is my job, crazy schedule and hours, might as well get used to it. "Sounds like fun, can't wait!"

Quickly I type in my name and number and hit save and hand her phone back to her. Moments later mine goes off with a text message.

"There, now you have mine. My schedule is a little crazy at the clinic but I have tomorrow off so maybe we can get together."

She turns and quickly starts heading for the door. "Sounds good," I manage just before she disappears, waving as she goes.

Again alone, I decide that today I'm going to take an inventory of all the supplies, that way I can keep tabs on what I use and when we need to restock pretty easily. This should take up a good portion of my day.

CHAPTER SIX

KADE

"You're late," my dad says without so much as looking at me when I walk onto the track.

"Sorry, silenced my phone last night and forgot to turn it back up, didn't hear the alarm."

"Kade, the excuses aren't going to help you win. We are all putting a lot of time and energy in this for you to win, I need to see the same out of you."

I hate when I feel twelve again around my dad. I get it, I messed up, it's not like I did it on purpose. "Dad, I'm working my ass off here as well. It's one time, it won't happen again."

"Between your times yesterday and being late today, there seems to be a pattern developing here."

I get it, I do. My dad has always told me if this is what I really want to do and I show them the dedication on my side, there isn't anything my parents wouldn't do to help me out and my dad has stayed true to that. He quit the job he had worked in for fifteen years to make sure I had everything I needed time wise on riding. He dove headfirst into the racing field, learning everything he could including the mechanics of the bikes. He could probably do a top end change better and faster than anyone else here. He even became my coach and now Cody's and I couldn't ask for a better one, but at moments like this it really sucks to have your father running everything.

Slamming the helmet onto my head, I strap the chin strap down and start up my bike. "Again, I'm sorry, won't happen again!" I shout over the rev of my bike.

If I explain why I had to silence my phone last night he will lecture me once again on the whole Brooke thing and honestly, I don't want to hear it. Neither of my parents care for her very much and I can't say that I don't understand their points, but my mom is waiting for me to find my soul mate or some crap like that so that I can think about settling down. Not something I'm looking at doing anywhere in the near future.

Taking off onto the track, I feel the tension draining from my body. Most people would probably think racing around a dirt track is boring, but there is nothing boring about it. It's competing to be the best, and feeling free and honestly a little terrified as you fly over the jumps, landing them and feeling exhilarated knowing you cleared it. I reach speeds up to forty-five and fifty miles per hour on some parts of this track and I don't think there is anything that feels freer than those moments. It's the only thing that truly calms me.

IT'S PRETTY warm today and the Texas sun is not letting up. Sweat is pouring down my face, my hands are soaked in my gloves and I've lost count of how many times I've been around the track. Turning the last corner, I see my dad waving me in.

Pulling off my helmet, my hair is soaked and plastered to my face. "How am I looking?"

"Better than yesterday for sure, but not up to your best yet."

He hands me a bottle of water. Half I drink, the other I dump over my head.

"Kade, why don't we take a break and grab some lunch, your mom just got back with food. We will take a few more runs a little later when things cool down a little out here."

Nodding my agreement, I follow him into the training center and down to the meeting room. Opening the door, I can smell the food that Mom brought in, but that is nothing compared to the electrical shock that goes through my body when I enter the room. What the hell is that all about? Looking around, I spot Cammie sitting at the table talking to Cody. Nothing prepares me for when she laughs and the feeling that shoots through me next. I have a need to punch Cody, then grab Cammie and pull her away. What is wrong with me today? I even find myself balling up my fist. Relaxing my hands, I sit at the opposite side of the table, away from Cammie. I'm exhausted, and probably a little dehydrated, those are the only reasons I can logically come up with for where my problem may lie right this minute.

"All right, now that everyone is here this is the best time to run over the agenda for this weekend's race. First off we need to leave tomorrow instead of Thursday. I don't want to push our time with getting up there. We will be driving straight through so we should get there in plenty of time this way to get everyone set and ready for Saturday's race. Any questions?"

Nothing but silence around the table. I find myself looking over at Cammie and feeling a little frustrated that she hasn't looked my way at all. I almost get the feeling that she is trying to ignore me on purpose.

"Cammie, have Kade show you the trailer and what we set up for you. I need you to check all the supplies today and make sure we have everything you may need. I'm running into town after we are done here to pick up some spare parts that we need so please make sure to contact me if there is something we don't have in the center. Cody and Kade, make sure all your gear is loaded today before you leave, we will check everything one last time before we head out tomorrow."

Looking over at Cammie, she is nodding her head but has her eyes directed down at a piece of paper she is writing on.

"I'll take her over as soon as we are done with lunch if that works for you, Cammie."

She looks over at me and nods. "Yes, thank you, Kade. That will be great." She instantly averts her eyes from me back to my father. "I'm sure we have everything here, you are pretty stocked up, but I'll contact you right away if I find anything so that you don't have to wait around in town for me."

"Don't worry about the time, I'll be there a while with the supplies that need to be picked up anyway," my dad assures her and the rest of what he says fades away.

I'm irritated and I don't know why. I want to jump up grab Cammie by the arm and make her look at me, but I'm not sure where that need comes from. Why do I care that she won't look at me? This morning when she was apologizing for yesterday, I know my reaction bothered her. I knew the moment she went from embarrassed to pissed. Her body language told me everything. She was leaning against her desk, her knuckles white from the grip she had on it, but the moment I told her it was no big deal she stood straight up, squared her shoulders and her eyes lit up with fire. It took everything in me to not lunge forward and calm her lips once again. Then I wanted to punch myself for even feeling that need, why is this woman having this kind of effect on me? Why is it that I want to keep far away from her but pull her to me at the same time?

"Kade? Kade!" My mother's voice breaks through my thoughts.

"Sorry! What?"

"What is with you today? You have been off all day. She asked you if Lucas will be joining us this weekend." My dad looks irritated and I get it, he is right. I've been off all day, starting with waking up two hours late.

Cammie is looking over at me now from the corner of her eye. There is a small smile on her lips, she's enjoying the wrath I'm receiving from my dad. I have a deep need to go and grab her up, pull her out of the room, to anywhere else where there isn't an audience, and kiss the hell out of her.

"Kade, what the hell is wrong with you?" Dad's voice booms through the room.

"No, he won't be joining us on this one he said," I answer his previous question, fully ignoring his last one.

My mom is sitting next to Cammie and I watch her as she looks between myself and Cammie and then back and a small smile stretches across her lips. I have to hold myself back from yelling at her not to go there, I've seen that smile before. She's thinking of grandchildren.

I need to get out of here but I have just agreed to take Cammie out to the trailer and show her what is what and all I'm wanting to do is get back on the track and run few laps without people around. A place where I can ignore everyone.

I've only taken a couple bites of my sandwich but I'm done and ready to get out of this room. "Cammie, are you ready? I have other things to do." I know I've snapped at her and I shouldn't have, she hasn't done anything, well aside from kissing me yesterday.

"Don't worry about it, if someone can send me in the right direction of the trailer I'm pretty sure I can find my way. I'd like to finish eating anyway." She closes her pen with a click and sets it on the notebook she was writing on, then grabs the half of her sandwich that hasn't been touched yet.

"No, you have to excuse my son..."

"Dad, I can speak for myself," I interrupt my dad from making an excuse for me. I don't know what is wrong with me. I do know I'm over this day and ready to go home already.

"I'm going to head out and get my gear together, when you're finished in here just meet me over at my room and I'll take you over there," I speak a little softer this time. She hasn't done anything and I don't know why I'm so irritated but I need a little time away from everyone.

"I won't be long, I promise, I know you have a lot to do to get ready to leave." She takes a large bite of her sandwich.

"Don't rush." Getting up, I grab my trash and dump it in the trash can as I head out the door, needing more than anything to get away from my mom's stare. I know what's going through her head, it's written all over her face. I need air!

CHAPTER SEVEN

CAMMIE

The door closes and I keep my eyes down on my food. I know everyone in the room is looking at me right now and I'm pretty sure if I look up they will know something happened between the two of us, even if it was just a kiss. This morning, after we talked and I apologized and how he acted, I thought I was worrying over nothing and it meant nothing to him. His reaction just now has me confused. He almost seems mad at me and I'm unsure why. There is a part of me that wants to take my time, but I know I shouldn't poke at him anymore and should quickly finish my lunch and get him to take me to the trailer and get it all over with.

"Cammie, please excuse my son," Michael starts to apologize for Kade.

I wave him off. "Don't worry, I'm sure he is under pressure with the race this weekend and everything. I know not to take it personally." I hope he doesn't see through my lie, I'm pretty sure the attitude he has, I'm involved with some way.

"Cammie, honey, I would take you myself but I need to run into town and get all the food for the weekend. We take the motorhome so that everyone has a place to relax during the races and since we moved up the time to leave I'm a little behind." Tracy tries to look sorry but something is telling me she isn't sorry at all that she isn't able to take me and that Kade has to.

I saw the way she was looking between her son and me, something tells me she is wanting Kade and me to spend a little time together. Here I was worried about being fired and I'm pretty sure Tracy would have been excited.

"Don't worry about it, Tracy, it's all good. I'm pretty sure I could handle this on my own if someone would just point me in the direction of the trailer," I try once again so that I can just go alone.

I felt the electricity that shot through my body the moment he walked into the room earlier, I'm pretty sure I don't need to be in the close confines of a trailer. I keep trying to figure out why he is causing this reaction in me, it's crazy. I need to shake this, whatever you want to call it, for Kade. There is nothing special about him and he's proven that every time we've been in a room with each other, but that kiss from yesterday flashed into memory as soon as I saw him. Today during this fun conversation between him and his dad, he once again flexed his jaw, this time out of anger. I still found myself adjusting in my seat, it was the sexiest thing and my palms itched to touch him again. I need to get over this, but damn if that isn't the sexiest thing and when Kade does it something inside of me gets set on fire.

"No, he needs to stop being a spoiled brat and help out a little." Tracy talks about him like he is a little boy, it's kind of cute.

Grabbing my trash, I get up from the table. "I need to make a quick phone call and then I will have Kade show me the room in the trailer to get the inventory, but I'm pretty sure, Michael, that I have everything. You have stocked this place pretty well, if it's not in there I'm sure it's in the supply room. I made a list of everything we have so I'll take my tablet."

"You have been busy. Sorry about the short notice for this weekend," Michael apologizes.

I wave him off. "You warned me about the hours and what to expect with this job, it's all good. I do have some questions, though, since we are driving do I take my own car, or do we follow each other? Exactly how does this work and who do I call for a hotel room? Do you guys already have rooms in a hotel there? I'd like to stay at the same one."

"We have really failed in the information department with you, haven't we?" Tracy looks over with a slight flush to her cheeks, almost like she is embarrassed. "We have the rig and trailer that is leaving tonight. Tomorrow morning everyone will meet here at normal time. Michael and I are taking the motorhome and then usually Kade takes his truck. Everyone who is going splits up between riding with us or Kade. We lock the gates when we leave so the cars are all good here while we are gone. As for your room, we have already booked you one so don't worry about that. Everything is covered under the team account."

Wow, all right. "Okay, I will meet you guys here in the morning then. I'm excited, I've never been to a race of any kind."

I'M NOT REALLY ready for my one-on-one guided tour of the team trailer so I decide to go back to my office real quick and make a phone call to my dear friend Lucas. I want to know what his involvement with this team is since Michael asked Kade if he would be joining us this weekend. I know he wouldn't be going as just the team cheerleader.

Flopping down in my office chair, I pull up his number on my phone and press the call button. Two rings and this time he actually answers his phone.

"Cammie, how is everything going?"

"Well, I just found out I'm going to Las Vegas tomorrow, but here is my question, why would they have asked if you were going? Exactly how do you know this family?"

Yesterday I had so many questions for my dear friend, but by the time we finally talked last night all I wanted to do was hide somewhere and not talk to anyone.

"I guess you can say I'm one of the on-call mechanics now. I met the family a few years back. Kade and I have a mutual friend. He invited me to one of the races to check it out and I became kind of hooked. He introduced me to Kade and we became instant buds. I started going to more and more of the races and started picking up the mechanics through Michael, there isn't anything that man can't fix on a bike. You know me, I've always worked on my own cars and this was pretty similar. At one of the races, the mechanic they had at the time didn't show up, I jumped in to help and well, the rest is kind of history, I guess you can say. Now when they go I usually go as one of the mechanics but unfortunately I couldn't get this weekend off, we are already shorthanded so I have to sit this one out."

When you meet Lucas, you would never guess his love for working on cars. He is always dressed top-notch, hair perfectly styled and not a sign of grease anywhere on his hands, but if he is home most likely his head is under the hood of his car, so it doesn't surprise me that he became interested in the bikes as well.

"So how did I come up for this job?"

"We were all out for a beer after one of the races and Michael made a comment that he was in need of someone in sports medicine for the team. Kade's grandmother had more money than I think the president has, it was nuts. I think her husband was in oil or something. Anyway, she wanted the best for her only grandson so they built that amazing training center you are in. I instantly thought of you, knowing you were almost done with school so I made the suggestion, you kind of know the story from there."

"Why didn't you tell me more about this place?" I know I asked this last night when I talked to him but I wasn't really in the right frame of mind last night either, I had a lot going on.

"Why didn't you ask more questions? Are you not liking it?"

"No, everything is fine. I know you knew I thought I was coming to work for a bull rider. Why didn't you ever mention it was a race team?"

I hear him laugh through the phone and I roll my eyes. "Cammie, you need to learn not to assume. I won't lie, yes, I knew what you were thinking, I'll admit I would have loved to have been there yesterday when you realized it wasn't what you thought. I knew when you were calling yesterday it was because you wanted to know why I hadn't said anything so I ignored it. I figured you would meet the team and be good with the job even if there isn't a fine bull rider for you to work with. How did the first meeting with Kade go?"

Which part? I think to myself. *The first time we met and I couldn't take my eyes off of him or the first time I worked on him and I couldn't keep my lips off of him,* I'm tempted to scream out. I know we are best friends but there are some things I think I need to keep to myself right now. Especially since they are friends as well, it may be a little different if Lucas didn't know Kade. Although Kade could be the one to say something to him and then he'd wonder why I didn't. Damn, how is one kiss screwing with my head this much?

"What can I say about Kade? He thinks he is God's gift to women, but I'm sure that's more of a front, but then again I have met the little piece that hangs onto his arm." I think back to the girl that was with him yesterday when I first met him and wonder how I can be remotely attracted to a guy that would prefer that type of woman.

"Ahh, so you met Brooke already. I have no idea what that's all about, I think more of a convenience thing than anything else. I'm a little surprised she was there, Michael hates having her hang out at the track and he doesn't keep that a secret either."

I got the feeling yesterday that Michael wasn't a huge fan of the girl. "Not sure, only met her for maybe a minute and to be honest it was enough, but I'm not here to judge."

"I have to go, we need to get together when you get back, though."

My phone starts to beep with another call coming through, looking at it I see Sam's picture on my screen. "Okay, I'll give you a call when we get back."

"Cammie, give Kade a chance, he really is a great guy."

"I'm here to do a job and my opinions on the riders isn't really important to do that so I'm sure everything will be fine." Now if only I believed my own words.

Lucas laughs again and I want to know why but my phone beeping with Sam's call reminds me she is there and I need to talk to her. "All right, I'll talk to you later. Bye."

Before he can say anything else, I swipe the screen to answer Sam's call. "Sam, how are things going? I miss you so much and have so much to tell you."

Sniffling is all I get from the other end of the phone. "Sam, are you all right? Are you crying, what's wrong?" I shoot the questions out all at once.

"I can't do this, Cammie, I can't tell him." She sounds defeated, which to know her is why this is breaking my heart.

Sam is my best friend from college and right before we graduated she found out her life was going to involve a couple of people she wasn't expecting, including her sister-in-law's older brother. Up until that time she was a rock, now she seems almost lost.

"Sam, it's all going to be all right, but you are going to need to tell him, hon, especially if his sister knows."

She sniffs loudly in the phone and I have to pull it away from my ear. "Cammie, I'm not going to be able to handle it if he doesn't care."

"Sam, that's not going to happen, I would put money on it, but you are the one who needs to make that decision. You already know my feelings on the subject."

Silence stretches over the phone, all I hear are her sighs. The door to the training center opens and Kade walks in. He looks over at me in the office and I put a finger up, asking him to give me just a second.

"Look, Sam, unfortunately I'm at work right now and not really able to talk, let me call you back tonight when I get off."

"That's right, you started your new job. Definitely call me back, I want to hear all about it, and real quick, is he cute?"

"This is something we are going to have to talk about later. Love ya, I'll call you later." I hang up before she can say anything else.

Quickly standing, I shove my phone in my back pocket and join Kade. "Sorry, I had a couple of quick phone calls to make first."

He shrugs and turns to head out of the room. "It's no biggie, just thought I'd see if you were ready. I finished getting my stuff together, figured I'd take it out since we were heading that way."

Wow, what an attitude change. When he left the lunch room earlier he was mad and irritated, now he seems like nothing was wrong earlier. This guy has some mood swings.

"Yes, I'm ready, just let me grab my tablet first so I can take the inventory." Running back into my office, I grab the tablet out of my drawer and quickly get back. I don't want to risk pissing him off again.

I follow him out of the building and to a golf cart waiting outside. In the back of the cart is a pile of riding gear. I don't say a word, I just round the cart and sit down in the passenger seat. He gets in next to me and we start around the building to a back lot that I didn't even know existed, this place seems never-ending.

Sitting there is a big rig and trailer, the trailer is purple and green and has the words 'Sandy Racing' written large on both sides along with a picture of two riders, who I'm going to say is safe to assume are Cody and Kade, probably one of the pictures Krystal took. Sitting next to the semi is a bus, which I'm guessing is the motorhome they were talking about at lunch. It's all very impressive to look at, no cost was spared when this was all put together.

Pulling alongside the trailer, Kade jumps out and starts grabbing stuff out of the back.

"Can I help carry something?" I come up alongside of him.

"Thank you," is all he says as he hands me what I believe is a chest plate and boots.

I wait as he grabs everything else and then follow him over to a door at the side. Balancing everything in one arm, he pulls the keys out of his pocket and unlocks the door. Pulling it open, he steps aside and allows me to enter first.

I have to keep the shocked expression off my face at the gentlemanly gesture, something I wasn't really expecting. "Thank you," I mumble as I climb the stairs and enter the trailer.

It's dark and I can see very little from the light entering through the door. I take a step inside but I'm not sure where to go, I can make out a narrow walkway to my left and what looks like maybe a room or something to my right. The heat from Kade's body as he steps into the trailer surprises me as his chest is against my back. Closing my eyes, I take a deep breath. This is insane, I can't have these feelings toward him, it's crazy how my body reacts to him.

He reaches around in front of me where there is a wall and flips on the light switch, lighting up everything in the trailer. I need to move, let him enter the trailer. I need to not make an ass out of myself again. What is it about this guy that causes me to lose all control of body and mind? It's a little unnerving.

CHAPTER EIGHT

KADE

Earlier when I got back to my room after lunch, I felt like an idiot. I didn't need to act like a jerk to Cammie, she hasn't done anything wrong, but my dad had been riding me since I got here and it was starting to rub me wrong. I used the time to gather my gear, load it up and by the time I went to the training center to see if she was ready, I was calm again.

She has said very little to me but I can't blame her so I don't push her on the way over here to the semi. Now I'm pressed up against her back to turn the light on and I have to fight the urge to drop everything I'm holding and wrap my arms around her waist, pulling her tighter to me. I don't care what she said today when she apologized for kissing me yesterday, she is just as affected right now as I am. I heard the deep intake of breath she took, what the hell is this woman doing to me? We need to get this over with so that I don't do something I'm going to regret later.

"Go to your left," I instruct. The moment she steps away from me a coldness overcomes my body and I have the need to loop my arm around her waist and pull her back up against me. Instead, to reassure I don't do anything to make this any harder, I shift some of my gear into my empty arm. I can't grab her if my hands are full, right?

"Go down to the end, on the right is where we can unload all of this stuff, then we can check out the room you have to work in."

She nods and starts down the walkway, when she gets to the end and rotates to the left, she opens the door to the cabinet there. She steps aside and waits for me. I add my load to the gear that's inside and grab the stuff from her and place it inside.

"Wow, that's a lot of gear."

"We don't even use a quarter of it to be honest, it's all just in case. We have extra jerseys, pants, safety gear, boots, that kind of stuff, all there just in case."

"So exactly how does this all work?"

"You mean the races?"

She nods and looks around. This semi is a new addition to the crew, we were working out of a much smaller truck before, more like a moving truck size. This thing is outfitted for just about everything.

"This race is a two-day race. We will run on both days, we have a practice lap and then a thirty-minute race. We have a sighting lap as well where we go out and ride over the track, kind of like an inspection I guess you can say. It's the start of the season so depending on how we do on each race we get points. At the end of the season, the one with the most accumulated points is number one." I give her the short version of the rules.

"I spoke to Lucas a little about it, I'm excited to see what this sport is all about."

She will not look at me, she just keeps looking around as she talks. "Come on down here, this is your area."

Walking back toward the door where we came in, on the other side is the door to the room. I open it and step aside.

"Here it is. Right here behind me is like a living room. We

have a television, couple of chairs, a couch, just a small area to hang in between the runs. This door is the bathroom."

This trailer is huge, but with the setup of everything it's not easy for two people to move around together in here. As she enters the room, I fill in the doorway and watch as she looks around. There are cabinets at the front of the room, a table for her to work on in the middle. Good thing she is little so that she can easily move around. Sitting against the end of the room is a desk area and a stool that she can move around to use.

"It's small in here." I really haven't been in here yet, this will be the first time out on a race with the semi.

She walks over and opens the cabinets, which are stocked tight. "It will work just fine. If it's anything that extreme then you will be in a hospital."

She opens up the last cabinet and bottles and boxes come falling out of it, she screams and covers her head. I leap forward, trying to catch the stuff falling out before more hits her.

"Cammie, are you all right?" My arms are full of bottles, bandages and I'm not sure what else, but it has stopped falling out. She is holding her forehead.

Dropping everything, I pull her hand away from her head. "Damn it, you're bleeding."

Looking down, there is a box laying on the floor at her feet, the corner must have gotten her. In the cabinet are some towels, I grab one and place it against her forehead.

"Let me sit down for a minute, I'll keep pressure on it for a moment then check it out." She sounds so calm.

"Cam, we should probably take you to the hospital."

"Kade, relax, I'm all right. Let me keep pressure on it for a minute and then I'll look at it."

She tries to push my hand away from the towel. "Cam, just relax, I have this."

Keeping the pressure on her head, I make my way around the

other side of the table and wrap my other arm around her waist, pulling her back against my chest. "Relax against me, I've got you."

Surprisingly, she doesn't fight me. She leans back and rests her head against my shoulder. She may be acting all tough and in control but her eyes are closed tight, she is hurting.

"Cam, please let me take you to the hospital, what if you need stitches?"

She slightly shakes her head side to side, her eyes tighten closed a little more. "Just give it a minute."

After a moment, I pull the towel away and blood begins to pour from the nice size opening just above her left eye. Reaching over, I grab another towel from the cabinet and switch it out. "I'm not waiting, we are going."

Pulling my phone out of my pocket, I pull up Cody's number.

It rings twice and he thankfully answers. "Hey, man, what's up?"

"Are you still here at the center?"

"Yes, why?"

"Look, Cammie and I are out at the semi. Cammie opened a cabinet and everything fell out and one of the boxes hit her on the head. She is bleeding pretty bad, I need to get her to the hospital. My truck keys are on the table next to the couch in my room, can you bring them out to me?"

"Damn, yeah, I'm on my way. Should we call for an ambulance instead?"

"No, I think we are good to take her."

Cammie hasn't said a word, she isn't fighting me and that confirms that it's bad enough for some medical attention. "Hey, are you awake?"

She nods. "Um hummm."

"I'll admit, I'm a little surprised you aren't fighting me a little more on this." I want to keep her talking to me.

"I see the towel you just took off my head, I agree I may need to get this checked." She points at the towel I had on her head first that is sitting next to her, bright red covers a large portion of the towel and the one I'm holding has blood already seeping through it.

She tries to sit up but moans again. "Hey, relax. Cody will be here in a minute."

It takes Cody maybe five minutes but I finally hear my truck pull up. Cody is in the doorway of the tiny room quickly.

He looks around and sees the towel on the table next to Cammie. "Damn, what the hell fell on her?"

"I think the corner of a box hit her. Here, help me stand her up and then maneuver her out of this trailer, we don't have a lot of room to work with, but I don't think she can walk without some help."

"Come on, Cammie, I got you." Cody's voice is soothing and tender and she wraps her arm around his shoulders as he helps her stand up.

I have to fight the urge to punch him and pull her back to me. What the hell is wrong with me? I know the only intention Cody has is to help. He leads her out of the trailer and very carefully down the stairs.

"Cam, do you think you can sit in the seat all right alone?" I'm not sure, she seems pretty wobbly but she only nods again. I pull the passenger door open and run around the truck to the driver's side, hopping in and sliding over to help Cody get her into my raised cab.

"Do you want me to ride with you?" Cody asks as he hands me the seatbelt.

"I think we got it. Call Dad, let him know what happened and tell him to get someone in there tonight to put nets up in the cabinets so this can't happen again."

"Got it." Cody shuts the door and I look over at Cammie. She has her face turned away from me, holding the towel to her head.

"Hey, are you all right?"

She again just nods. "Cam, look at me."

"I can't."

"Why?"

"If I turn my head I'm afraid I'll get blood on your seat."

She's worried about my damn seats, seriously? "Look at me, I want to see your eyes, please."

"Kade, please just go. I'm fine, I promise."

There is that stubborn side. Surprisingly it makes me feel a little better if she is arguing with me.

IT TAKES ABOUT twenty minutes to get to the hospital, I pull into the parking lot. "Let me find a wheel chair, I'll be right back."

She unhooks her seatbelt and reaches for the door. "I don't need a wheelchair, I can walk." She starts to step down from my truck, I throw myself out of the driver's side and run around the front just in time to catch her as she misses the step.

"Damn it, Cammie, wait for some help. You probably have a concussion as well, stop being so stubborn."

I go to pick her up and she pushes away from me. "You are not going to carry me in. Relax, I'm fine, I can walk."

"Man, you're pigheaded." I walk alongside her, ready to catch her the moment she starts to sway. She makes it inside without any problems.

"Go sit down, I'll get you checked in." To my surprise she doesn't argue.

Walking over, the lady sitting behind the counter looks up. "Can I help you?"

"Yes, that lady sitting over there has a head injury, possible stitches."

She hands me a clipboard and a pen. "Have her fill this out, we can get her right in."

"Thank you." Walking over, I sit down next to Cammie and hand her the paperwork.

"Here, fill this out and then they will take you right back."

Cammie fills out the forms and gets up from the chair. "Kade, I appreciate all your help, but I'll call my parents and they will come down to pick me up."

"I'm not going anywhere, just go get your head checked," I snap back at her.

"Kade..."

"Stop arguing with me, Cammie, I'm not going anywhere. Do you want me to go back with you?"

She just shakes her head and turns to the lady at the desk, handing her the clipboard. I can't hear what's being said between them but when I see the lady get up and open the door for Cammie to go back, I have to fight the urge to get up and follow her.

As the door shuts behind her I lean forward, my elbows on my knees, my face in my hands. I'm not sure why I feel so possessive over this woman. When Cody pulled her away from me I wanted to pull her back and tell him to back off. I wanted to tell him to drive my truck while I held her on the way over here and then she mentioned she would call her parents to come and pick her up and I wanted to take the phone away from her so she had no way to call them. This isn't right and I don't have time for it either. Maybe it's a better idea if her parents come and take care of her from here. Grabbing my phone out of my pocket, I scroll through and find Lucas's number. He will know how to get ahold of her parents to come pick her up.

My finger lingers over Lucas's number, this is a distraction I don't need right now and the more I'm around her the more I'm realizing I don't want to leave her. The kiss from yesterday comes to mind and the way I felt when our lips met, I didn't want to let go.

Before I can change my mind again I press call and wait.

"Hey, Kade, what's up?"

"Hey, man, Cammie had a little accident today and I'm here with her at the hospital."

"What the hell happened, is she all right? I'm on my way."

"Lucas, relax." What is their relationship with each other? He seems a lot more concerned than just her being a friend.

"We were in the semi checking out supplies, she opened a cabinet and a bunch of stuff fell out, a corner of a box came down and cut her forehead open above her left eye. It was bleeding pretty good and I wanted to make sure she didn't have a concussion so I brought her in. She is back with the doctor now, but I have a ton of stuff to get done before tomorrow. I was wondering if you could get ahold of her parents, I don't have any information on them, and have them come down to get her."

"I'm already on my way, I'll be there in about ten minutes. I'll call her parents and let them know what's going on."

I want to tell him never mind, I'll take care of her, but I know that I need to walk away. "All right, I'll wait until you get here."

CHAPTER NINE

CAMMIE

I have no idea how long I have been sitting here in this exam room but the doctor seems to be taking his time getting to me. All this waiting is giving me way too much time alone to think. Thinking back to the trailer as Kade stood there holding me while we waited, I felt protected in his arms. Yes, I may have been bleeding from the head profusely but I felt safe. When Cody pulled me away from the safety of Kade's arms I wanted to fight my way back into them. The ride over here, it was hard to not slide over to his side and ask him to hold me. This can't be more than being grateful for him being there and helping me through all of this, I can't be falling for the moody rider that I'm working for. The guy that believes a woman is just a toy to hang onto his arm and be at his beck and call. How can I know all of this about him and still find myself fighting the attraction I feel toward him?

I feel this because today he showed me the side of him that's not the player, the tender side, and even though he did snap at me when I mentioned calling my parents it wasn't out of anger, I saw the frustration in his eyes.

The doctor enters and draws my attention back to my throbbing head. After about twenty questions and him poking and probing, it is decided that I need stitches and have a slight concussion. With eight stitches and directions to not drive for the evening, I finally walk out of the room an hour and a half later.

Walking into the waiting room and not seeing Kade but Lucas is a surprise. Why did he snap at me if all he was planning on doing was calling someone himself to come and pick me up? Maybe I read him wrong and he is mad at me.

"There's my girl, how are you?" Lucas hops up from his chair, his eyes going to the large bandage around my head.

One thing about doctors that drives me crazy. Instead of the square bandage he could have used, he wrapped my head up like I just had surgery or something.

"I'm good, eight stitches, but he assured me I'm all good to go, just no driving for the rest of the day. Problem is the only thing I have on me is my phone, I left everything else in my office at work."

Lucas looks down at his watch. "Well, it's only five, so I'm sure someone is still at the center, especially since you guys leave tomorrow. We can stop by there first and then I can take you home. Your car can stay there, I'm sure your mom or dad can drop you off in the morning, then it's there when you guys get back."

If Kade is still there I'm not sure I want to see him. I read him so wrong today and I'm pretty sure I don't have the energy for anything he may want to throw at me, especially his sarcasm.

"I'm sure everything is fine there until tomorrow, I'm ready to be home to be honest. I'll just grab it all in the morning."

"Are you sure? I can even drop you off at home first and then go back for everything."

Nodding, I head for the door to exit the hospital. "It's all good, but thank you."

Lucas puts his arm around my shoulders and pulls me into his side as he directs me over to his car. "Anything for you and you know it."

THE MOMENT we pull into the driveway, Mom and Dad come out the front door and my phone starts going off. I find myself feeling disappointed when I look down and see Krystal's name on my screen.

"Hey, Krystal, I just pulled up to my house. Let me get inside and answer the hundred questions I'm seeing all over my mom's face and I'll call you back."

"All right, but first, you are okay, right?"

"Yes, I'm all good, give me a few minutes and I'll call you back."

"Don't forget about me." Then the line goes quiet.

The door to Lucas's car is pulled open by my mom. "Honey, are you all right?"

"Mom, the bandage looks worse than it is, only a few stitches."

"How many is a few?" She grabs my arm to help me out of the car and grabs my elbow to lead me to the house.

"Eight, I believe."

"That's not a few, Camille."

Lucas and my dad follow us into the house, my mom leads me to the living room and has me sit down in the recliner. "What happened?"

The three sit there and listen as I tell the shortest version of what happened as possible with the hopes that it will answer all of the questions.

"Cody called Michael and they should have it all fixed before we leave tomorrow."

"Wait! Leave for where? Should you be going anywhere?" Mom's voice rises with concern.

I just found out about this weekend today and I haven't been home until now to tell my parents about it.

"They have a race this weekend in Las Vegas, we leave tomorrow. I just found out about it this morning."

"Did the doctor say it was all right to go?" Dad asks, looking concerned.

"All he said is not to drive tonight just in case I have a slight concussion. I won't be driving tomorrow, we go up with the team so all I will really be doing is sitting anyway. I'll be fine. I just need one of you to take me to work in the morning, my car is still there."

I can see it in both of their eyes, they want to argue with me and demand I not go but they know they can't and this is my job. I need to be there.

"Trust me, once I change this huge bandage out you will see it's not as bad as it looks right now," I try to reassure them both.

The rest of the evening I spend packing and calling everyone back. Krystal offers to come pick me up in the morning and I take her up on the offer, this way my parents can't try and talk me out of going all the way to work.

Michael calls and assures me that everything is taken care of in the cabinets so that something like this can't happen again and repeatedly apologizes for it happening the first place, even Tracy calls and asks every question my mom has asked me, it must be a parent thing. There hasn't been anything from Kade. I'm disappointed but convince myself it's for the best, I need to stop reading so much into this and realize he is a player and any human would have done what he did when something like this happens to another person.

THE NEXT MORNING I change out the bandage and realize the bruise covering the whole left side of my eye, across my forehead and reaching down to my cheek isn't helping my case in trying to convince my parents I'm good to go with the team. Normally they wouldn't have been up as early as I am, but of course they have to make sure for themselves that I'm all good. It doesn't help that when I open the door when Krystal comes to pick me up her eyes go wide and she startes fussing over me.

"Guys, it looks a lot worse than it actually is, please understand I'm a grown woman and I know how to take care of myself."

Giving each of my parents a hug, I grab my bags before my dad can and basically shove Krystal out the door toward her car.

Pulling up to the center, I see the semi and the bus already pulled over and everyone is rushing around to get everything ready to go.

Cody meets Krystal on her side, opening the car door for her, he is such a sweetheart and a gentleman. That's the kind of guy a girl should be attracted to, not the temperamental playboy that I seem to not be able to stop thinking about.

"Good morning, ladies, I'll grab the bags and put them in Kade's truck." He gives Krystal a quick kiss.

I try to keep my face directed down to not draw attention to it, but as I turn Cody is now standing in front of me. "How are you feeling?" His eyes search my face.

"Only eight stitches." I try to play it off as no big deal, I'm not about to tell anyone how much my head is throbbing right now. If I were to say anything at home I'm sure my mom would have locked me in my room, here they may not let me go. By the time we get there I should be doing fine.

"Only eight stitches." His sarcasm isn't missed.

"I left all my stuff here last night so I need to run to my office real quick, I'll be right back."

I'm able to get to the training center without running into anyone else. In my office, I grab my purse from the floor next to my desk but when I stand back up the room begins to spin. "Damn it." Sitting down, I lay my head back against the back of the chair and close my eyes, willing the throbbing to go away and the room to stop moving.

"What's wrong?" I jump at the sound of the male voice.

Opening my eyes, I jump again when I find Kade standing right in front of me, his face only inches from mine.

"I'm fine." I try to push back to put a little space between us, but I have no where I can really go.

"Cammie, don't lie to me, I see the pain etched all over your face."

"I bent down to pick up my purse and stood up too fast is all."

He doesn't say anything, but his jaw clenches and I need him to back off. I grip the chair tightly to keep from grabbing him. I need space from him and now before I embarrass myself again. Pushing myself up, I figure it will push him back so I can step away from him, but no such luck, it just brings us chest to chest and he isn't moving. Instead his arm goes around my waist, and I look to the side to keep from looking at him.

"Stop lying to me, Cam, are you all right?" His breath is hot against my cheek.

"If you were that worried you'd think you would have stayed last night like you told me you were," I attacked back, needing space. My hands against his chest, I push him back, but he doesn't release me.

"We need to get going, Kade, please let me go."

"What are you doing to me, Cam?"

That brings my eyes to his, our lips are only inches apart. Yesterday after the box fell on me I noticed he started calling me Cam and I felt comfort in it then, now it's doing things to my insides that I shouldn't be feeling toward my boss.

"Kade, please, I'm not a trophy girl. I'm not someone who you can have around when you want to and then push me to the side when the mood isn't hitting you."

"You kissed me first," he throws back into my face.

"I know and I apologized for it a number of times, I have no explanation for it or excuse."

"So you regret kissing me?"

"Kade, you're my boss."

"That's not answering my question, Cammie."

There is no way I can tell him I regret it when we are this close together, he will see right through me. I only regret it because of the work situation. Do I actually regret the kiss? No!

Before anything else can be said, his lips claim mine. My hands instantly go from his chest to up around his neck, my fingers digging into his scalp at the back of his head. My body goes lax against him and the moan I hear is from me. I'm lightheaded but this time it has nothing to do with the stitches in my head.

His hand is at the small of my back and he presses me against him, I can feel the evidence of how he is affected by this kiss.

His lips leave mine and he trails kisses up to my right ear. "It was the hardest thing I have ever done, leaving you last night for another man to take care of."

"Why did you leave then?"

He pulls back and his eyes look a little confused. "I'm not one of those guys that feels possessive over a woman, never have, but then you walk into my life and for some reason all I want to do is take you and make you mine. This isn't the right time, though, I need to concentrate on racing right now."

Those words are like cold water being poured over my entire body. I step back, this time he releases me. "I just said I'm not one of the 'convenient girls,' Kade. I can't, I'm sorry. You concentrate on winning, I'll make sure you are healthy enough to be number one."

I don't want to hear anymore, I need space from him. I could easily became a convenience for him and that makes me sound so cheap and I hate myself for that. How can a guy have that kind of effect on me?

Grabbing my purse, I push past him and quickly out of the room. I hear his steps behind me, I just pray he doesn't touch me, because then my body disregards everything my brain says.

"Cam, wait."

Shaking my head, I just walk faster. My head is pounding and I need space.

"Cammie, I said stop." He is right behind me, if he really wanted me to stop he could stop me and that's what keeps me going.

Bursting through the door, the sunlight beams into my eyes, squinting against it isn't helping my head. Stopping, I feel like I'm going to throw up. I need to sit down. I take a couple more steps and my knees give way.

"Damn it, Cammie." Kade is there and I'm in his arms.

"I'm fine, please let go of me." This isn't helping, now all I want to do is wrap my arms around him and hold on tight.

"Cammie, are you all right?" Michael is running over to us, concern written all over his face.

"I'm good, just got a little dizzy when I came out to the light and was squinting. I just need to get my sunglasses out of my car I think." I try to pull away from Kade but his arms just tighten every time I try to push away.

"Are you going to be all right to go this weekend?" Michael asks.

"I'm good, I promise. The next two days are all driving so I won't be doing much anyways, I promise I'll rest, just a slight concussion."

"Kade, take her over to the bus, she can ride with us and lie down," Michael instructs.

"She is riding with me in the truck." Kade lifts me into his arms and starts toward the truck.

The look on Michael's face has mine flaming with embarrassment, I'm surprised when I catch the smile on the corner of his lips as he doesn't argue with his son but turns and heads to the bus himself. What just happened?

"Put me down, please. I can walk." I try to wiggle and get him to set me down, not my smartest idea and all it's doing is drawing more attention to us.

Nothing, he just keeps walking. I have never been more embarrassed. Everyone I work for is staring right now, professionalism just went right out the door. With one hand he opens the passenger side door of his truck and with an ease I'm not expecting, he lifts me up and places me on the seat.

"Give me your keys, I'll go get you sunglasses." He holds his hand out and waits.

"Kade, I can go and get my own glasses."

"Cammie! Keys!"

Rolling my eyes, I hand them over. He shuts the door to make sure I don't jump out of the truck or something. My head falls back against the seat and I close my eyes.

Moments later the door reopens. "Put these on and don't move." Kade throws the glasses onto my lap and without even giving me a chance to say thank you, he shuts the door again.

My temper starts to flare up, who does he think he is bossing me around? I want to open the door and jump out just to spite him but if I'm being completely honest with myself, I don't feel well and it feels good to lay my head back a little.

I jump when the door behind me opens and slams shut. "What was that all about? My cousin is never like that with women, what's going on between the two of you?" Krystal leans in between the two front seats, her face close to mine.

"Nothing is going on, I think he just feels guilty because he was with me when it happened is all." I try to sound causal.

"I have no idea who you think you are fooling, the chemistry between you two can be felt across the parking lot." She rests her elbows on the center console of the truck, her chin in her hands like she is waiting for the most exciting story of the day.

"I'm sorry to disappoint you but nothing is going on between Kade and myself so whatever you think you are seeing, it's all in your imagination." My head still resting against the seat, I turn to look out the window, hoping to end this conversation.

Instead I'm saved by the guys opening the doors to the truck to get in. "Cody, you can sit up here, I have no problem sitting in the back. You probably have more leg room up here."

"I'm good, Cammie, but thank you." He looks at the back of Kade's head and then back at me with a knowing smile.

Really, Cody, too?!

CHAPTER TEN

KADE

I had all intention of keeping my distance. The drive home from the hospital I had a conversation with myself, knowing I did the best thing by calling Lucas to come stay with Cammie last night, no matter what I felt. She is a distraction and I don't need one right now.

When I walked into her office this morning and saw her face it about broke me. I hated myself for leaving her and everything I told myself about staying away went out the door. I knew I should walk away before she realized I was there, but my feet went in her direction which is something my body seems to do every time I'm around her.

Then we kissed, this time it was all me, it was something I started and it felt right to have her in my arms, her fingers in my hair, her body pressed tight against mine. I've been with women and I've had no problem keeping it casual, but something with Cammie is different. She told me she wasn't going to be a convenience for me, a trophy girl as she put it, the thought almost made me laugh just knowing she must be doing a little research on racing to even know what a trophy girl is. I still pushed, trying to tell her I didn't have time and I needed to concentrate on racing, which was a dick move on my part. I was the one pushing and then I throw it in her face like she was pushing me. I let her go because of that. Watching her walk away from me, I realized she doesn't deserve the way I have been treating her and I needed to apologize, maybe try to clear it all up a little nicer, but she wasn't having any of it. Then she collapsed in the parking lot and all I knew was I needed to be the one there, her in my arms, me taking care of her. Fighting this thing between me and her isn't going to work. I was hoping to have the drive to talk to her, I forgot we wouldn't be alone in the truck, so the talking will have to wait.

"So where are we stopping tonight?" Krystal breaks through my thoughts.

"I think Dad said the New Mexico, Arizona border. We are traveling about ten hours today, then I think he said we will only have about six or seven tomorrow."

We have only been on the road for about an hour and Cammie fell asleep probably fifteen minutes into the drive.

"Should we wake her? She did say she has a slight concussion." Krystal leans forward and looks at Cammie from the back seat.

"No, don't wake her. I sure it's a healing process, it's been a busy morning," Cody pipes in from behind me, a hint of playful sarcasm in his voice.

"Yes, cousin, what was all that about anyway? I've never known you to be so possessive." I hear the laughter in Krystal's voice.

"How am I being possessive?"

"You are kidding, right? Uncle Michael tells you to take her to the bus so she can lie down through the drive and you basically caveman it and tell everyone she is riding in here with you, so again I ask, what's going on between you two?"

Looking over at Cammie, I realize I don't have an answer for my cousin. It's been there since the moment I met her. We had an instant attraction to each other and neither of us can deny it, but beyond that I have no answer.

Krystal places her hand on my shoulder and leans over toward me. "You can deny all you would like, Kade, but figure it out before it's too late. Cammie is great, nothing like those you like to bring around."

No one around here likes Brooke, I get it, they don't hide their feelings about her. I'm pretty sure they all would push any other woman at me if it got Brooke to be part of the past and stay there. If I'm honest with myself, I would be all right with it as well. Realizing that is one of the reasons why last night I finally answered her call and explained that now wasn't the time for me to be distracted and that I'm going to make sure racing comes first this season.

This was after my drive home and I had convinced myself I was staying away from Cammie as well. That didn't last long and I'm realizing it may be more of a distraction to stay away from her. I don't understand this attraction. She is beautiful, I'd have to be blind not to see that and she is very independent, she can stand on her own to two feet, but I've known lots of beautiful women. There is something else pulling me toward her.

"Krystal, something you will learn about me is I'm a very light sleeper." Cammie keeps her face toward the passenger window.

"Sorry, Cammie." My cousin sits back in her seat, a devilish smile on her face as she looks at me in the rearview mirror.

There isn't one ounce of her that is sorry, I'd put money on it.

"Cammie, how are you feeling?" Cody's question irritates me, because I wanted to be the one to ask. Damn this attraction to this woman, since when do I get jealous?

With her head still against the headrest, Cammie turns to look over her shoulder. "Better, thank you. Sorry I fell asleep on you guys, hope I didn't snore."

Only softly and barely audible, I think to myself. *I'd say it is more like small sighs, with a little moan.*

"Do you still feel dizzy?" I'm not about to let it seem like Cody is the only one who cares.

She shakes her head slightly. "No." Her answer is sharp, where when she answered Cody she was soft-spoken and friendly.

"You better get better in the next day or so because once we hit Vegas we have to hit up a couple dance clubs."

"Babe, no late nights, we have races to win," Cody pitches in before Cammie can answer Krystal.

"I'm aware of that, but it doesn't mean we can't go out and have a couple hours of fun, does it? Plus, who says you need to come along? We can do a girls' night out." Yep, there is my sassy cousin I know so well.

"Do you honestly think..."

"Krystal." Cammie interrupts Cody which is probably a good thing for him, Krystal isn't one to be bossed around well. "I'm not making any promises. If these bruises don't go away I may be hiding out all weekend long."

"Trust me, you don't want to hide all weekend. Before Cody and I got together, the best part of the racing was all the riders, trust me on that."

I look into the rearview mirror at my cousin and she smirks at me. I'm pretty sure I would have been all right with leaving her at home this weekend.

"Never know when you will meet someone," Krystal adds and throws her eyebrows up at me in the mirror.

I see Cammie look over at me then over her shoulder at my cousin. She isn't missing a thing, she knows exactly what Krystal is doing right now and she is actually entertained by it if the smile on her face is any indication of what's going on in her head.

Maybe I should have Cammie ride in the bus, because if Krystal is going to do this the whole drive there, I may end up pulling over and kicking her out of my truck. Better yet, maybe I should tell her and Cody they need ride in the bus for a while. On the flip side, if I did that it would only add fuel to Krystal's matchmaking skills.

"Cammie, Michael was telling me the other day that Lucas is the one who mentioned you for this job, how do you know him?"

Thank you, Cody, for a subject change. Plus, this is something I've been wanting to know myself.

"I've known Lucas since we were in the sixth grade. I was the new kid in class, starting in the middle of the year and making friends is hard at that age. I was shy then..."

"You're kidding, right?" There is no way this woman, the one who grabbed me and kissed me on the first day of meeting, could have ever been shy.

"I know, hard to believe. Anyway, it was probably after about two weeks of me eating by myself at lunch that one day he walked up and asked if he could sit with me. I honestly thought it was a joke being played on the new girl. Lucas was the popular kid, he always had a group of guys around him. When I didn't answer, he just sat down across from me and started eating his lunch. The whole time I sat there waiting for something to happen, but it didn't. The bell rang and he got up and left, we didn't say anything to each other the whole lunch. The next day he came over, only this time not asking, and sat down again with me. On day four, he finally broke the silence at the table between the two of us and starting asking me where I used to live, questions about my family and from then on we have been best friends."

"Did you guys ever take it further than best friends?" Krystal pops up between us again, leaning on the center console.

"How are you this close if you have a seatbelt on?" I look over at her with a knowing look.

"You are such a pain, how am I supposed to hear sitting back here?"

"Krystal, seatbelt now."

Cammie turns herself in the seat, her knees pulled up onto the seat as she leans around to look at Krystal. "No, we have never been anything more than best friends. I've had a couple boyfriends and him girlfriends that used the excuse they didn't believe we were only friends to break up with us, but we have never looked at each other that way. He is more like the big brother I never had and me the annoying little sister. We are both the only child of the family."

"If I didn't already know him as well as I do, I would say the man has to be gay." Cody voices exactly what I'm thinking.

Cammie laughs, and not just a small giggle but a real laugh, and it goes straight to my gut and then down to harder parts of my body. I adjust in my seat and realize nothing is making it any more comfortable.

"Trust me, he has been told a few times that he must be if he hasn't tried anything with me. He just laughs and lets them assume whatever they want to."

"I went on a couple dates with him," Krystal announces.

Cammie bends around her seat as much as the seatbelt will allow. "What? Are you serious?"

"Yep, it wasn't anything serious and I'm ashamed to say I only agreed to go because he had asked me in front of Cody and I had a huge crush on him and was trying to make him jealous."

"It worked, I have never wanted to punch a man as much as I wanted to Lucas when he asked her out for the second time. I finally manned up and asked her out myself." Cody leans across and kisses Krystal.

IT'S ABOUT one in the afternoon and we are finally pulling over at a tiny little diner in a very small little town for lunch. Dad called about twenty minutes ago letting us know that we were going to stop, swearing that the place might not look like much but had the best burgers around.

Pulling into the parking lot, I throw the truck into park and jump out. Rounding the front, I get to Cammie's door just as she opens it to jump out.

"Kade, I'm good." She still sounds frustrated with me.

Krystal and Cody have already gotten out of the truck and are walking over to the bus to meet up with everyone.

Cammie steps down and with my arms I trap her against the truck and passenger seat. "We need to talk."

Cammie looks to her right where everyone is standing around. "Really, we need to do this now? Haven't we caused reason enough for everyone to be talking? Krystal made it pretty clear what I'm sure everyone else is thinking. And you made it very clear that you weren't interested, but yet you keep doing stuff like this, Kade."

"Cam, I know this isn't the time or place, but we need to talk."

She stares at me for a moment, then takes a deep, defeated sigh. "Fine, we can talk, but not here, and not when we have everyone watching, please. So for now can you let me go?"

Pushing away from her, I step back enough for her to walk past me. Shutting the door, I turn and follow. Cody, Krystal and Kyle are in a little group talking, she quickly walks over to them and the four of them head over to the front door of the diner.

Walking up, my mom smiles and I can only imagine what is going through her head. She probably already has us having children. I roll my eyes and shake my head, basically telling her without words not to get involved. That just makes her smile bigger.

"Come on, Mom, let's go eat." I wrap an arm around her shoulders and we walk in together.

Walking up to the table, I notice Cammie has sat herself in between Krystal and Kyle already, I'm sure making it a point to not have to sit next to me. Sitting directly across from her, I can tell she is doing everything in her power not to look in my direction. She laughs at something Kyle says and I find that I'm a little bothered that she can have that kind of conversation with everyone but me. Now that I think about it, I'm pretty sure she has never laughed at something I said. Why that is bothering me I have no clue, but when I look up and see Kyle gently touching her cheek where she is bruised, I have to pull some self-restraint from somewhere or I am going to reach across, grab his arm and pull him across the table and punch, a couple of times.

Kyle is a great guy. He has been with us for a few months and is a great mechanic, next to Lucas we couldn't have anyone better on our team. I believe he is a year younger than me. A couple of years ago he was racing and another rider lost control of his bike and took Kyle out with him. He broke his back in two spots, along with his leg and arm. With the plates in his back he can no longer ride. He is great to have around, even helps out with training every once in a while. But if he touches Cammie one more time I may fire him on the spot and leave him here.

A hand under the table grabs mine and I jump. Looking to my left, my mom is shaking her head at me. I have got to get ahold of myself, this is crazy. Now I'm starting to piss myself off.

CHAPTER ELEVEN

CAMMIE

It's been a long day, getting into my room for the evening I lie down on the bed, covering my eyes with my arm. How can sitting in a car all day be this exhausting? The answer to that is pretty simple, Kade! This morning he kisses me, then basically pushes me away stating he doesn't have the time, then gets possessive and tells me we need to talk. If anything is making me dizzy it may be his mood swings.

I don't like playing games, but here I find myself playing them with Kade. When we stopped for lunch I made sure I sat where he couldn't sit next to me, I may have even flirted with Kyle a little and now I feel ashamed. Using Kyle isn't fair and I need to get my head back on straight. This could all go bad really fast.

I jump when someone knocks at my door. Kade said we needed to talk, but I'm not really feeling up to that talk right now. Maybe if I just lie here, whoever it is will go away. Another knock, a little harder this time.

Moaning, I get up and walk over.

"Cammie, you all right?" Krystal's voice comes through the door before I can get there.

She sounds worried, I can't not answer it now. Opening it, I find her and Cody standing there.

"One more knock and I would have called someone to come open it." She waves her hand up around the side of my face.

"Sorry, I was lying down."

"Are you all right?" Cody now looks concerned.

"Just a little headache, nothing I don't expect. I have eight stitches in my head and I look like someone used the side of my head as a punching bag," I tease, trying to lighten the mood.

"We are all heading down to dinner, we told Michael we would grab you on the way down."

"I think I'm going to skip, tell them thank you, though." I'm tired and really don't have the energy to deal with Kade right now.

"Are you sure? Want us to bring you something on our way back up?" Cammie offers.

I am about to say no but then realize I can't take my pain medicine without something in my stomach first. "Do you mind grabbing me some kind of salad? I'm not real picky, just no onions please, if they have a chicken caesar that sounds pretty good. If not, anything with ranch dressing, please."

"Anything to drink? Are you sure you don't want to come down?"

"I'm good, I have a couple bottles of water in here, I'm just going to relax, but thank you."

Krystal wants to argue with me, I see it written in her eyes, but Cody leads her away by the arm. "All right, we will get you something. If you need anything everyone has a phone, just give someone a call."

I watch as they walk down the hallway to the elevator. Closing the door, I walk over to my purse, remembering I have a granola bar and that should hold me over so that I can take my pain meds. My head is pounding.

After taking something for my head, I lie down and close my

eyes. If it doesn't take long for the meds to work, maybe I'll think about going down with the others. I don't want them thinking I'm anti-social or something.

THROUGH THE FOG I can hear someone calling my name but I can't figure out who it is. There is a pounding, but I'm not sure where it's coming from. The voice gets louder, that's when I realize this isn't a dream. Damn, I must have fallen asleep.

Slowly opening my eyes I look around, but I don't hear anything now, maybe it was a dream. I do hear some muffled noises in the hallway, then I hear the lock at my door. What the heck, someone is coming in!

Quickly getting up, I make it to the door just as it flies open and Kade comes barreling in. "Kade, what the hell are you doing? How did you get a key to my room?"

He stops in the doorway and just stares at me like I have grown a second head or something. His confused look turns pissed. I know that look all too well when it comes to Kade, I have been on the receiving end of it way too many times in the last couple of days.

"Is everything all right, sir?" I hadn't noticed the hotel employee until now.

Kade doesn't say a word, he just stares at me.

"I'm sorry for any confusion, sir, everything is good in here, thank you," I answer the poor guy standing there looking very confused, it looks like he may be a manager.

I watch as he looks me over then looks at Kade like he is waiting for the all okay.

Kade takes a deep breath and turns to the man standing in the hallway. "Thank you for coming so quickly." He shakes the guy's hand and without waiting for him to respond he shuts the door.

"Kade, what the hell is going on?"

He doesn't say anything, he is just standing there staring at me. I can see the different emotions soaring through his eyes, relief, anger, and then something else I'm not quite sure how to describe.

"Kade!" I try again.

"Why didn't you answer the door?" He takes a step toward me, I take one back.

"I was asleep, I was on my way to open it when you came barging in."

"I have been standing outside of your room for ten minutes, pounding on the door and calling out your name, Cam."

"So you decided to call down to the front desk and have someone come up and open the door?"

There is the anger again and I want to take another step back, but I hold my ground.

"Krystal said you weren't feeling well, I was bringing you up some dinner."

I look down and see nothing. He doesn't have food with him, so I give him a questioning look.

"Damn it, Cam, you scared the hell out of me!" he yells at me and closes the space between us. His arm goes around my waist as his hand digs into the hair at the back of my head and his lips claim mine. This shouldn't be happening, but there isn't an inch of my body that is agreeing with me. Instead my arms are going around his waist, pulling him tighter against me.

I know where this is going and that should be enough for me to push away from him. We kiss, he gets all moody, I feel guilty and we storm apart from each other. Besides the fact that he is my employer, which should be reason enough.

His tongue finds mine and every thought is lost. I can feel his hardness pressing tight against his jeans, and my hands itch to reach down. I don't realize I'm being walked back until the backs of my legs hit the edge of the bed. I sit down onto the edge and he follows me, one arm going to the bed behind me to brace himself, the other now cradling my head as he gently lays me down. Scooting myself up farther onto the bed, he follows me.

He gently runs a finger over the bruised side of my face. It's so light I almost don't feel it. Kade has a tender side!

"Two days ago you kissed me and something shifted. I have tried fighting it, but every time I'm around you it's more work to keep my hands off you than not. I need to be concentrating on the race, but I'm realizing being away from you might be mentally taking me away from it more than having you at my side. I know you are strong and you can take care of yourself and when Krystal told us you decided to skip dinner I figured you were trying to prove some point, but when you weren't answering your door the worst scenarios ran through my mind and I needed to get to you. I have no idea what you are doing to me, but I know fighting it isn't working."

I need to say something but I'm in too much shock to talk. I have questions for him and myself. I think the most important one I need to ask myself right now is this—it worth this not working and losing my job? He is right, though, fighting whatever this is between us isn't working.

"Cam, I see the wheels turning in your head."

"I like it when you call me Cam, no one has ever called me that." I finally find my voice. "Kade, I love this job, I may have only been here a couple days but this is what I wanted to do when I decided to go into this profession, to work privately for an athlete. To have this fall right in my lap right out of school is unheard of. I'm not going to deny I'm attracted to you, but I can't lose this job."

"I'm suggesting we see where this goes, stop fighting each other."

"Your dad..."

"They all see it, Cam, if it was going to be a problem he would have already voiced his opinion. Trust me on that, my family isn't shy."

"So what? You want to jump right into this? I already told you, Kade, I'm not one of those girls you can sleep with when you have a need and push me aside when the mood isn't there."

He rolls over to his side, propping himself up on his arm. "That's not what I'm saying I want, Cam. I'm not promising forever or anything, I'm saying I'd like to see what this is between us."

The sensible side of my brain is yelling at me to say no. Send him back to his room and tell him I'm a professional and hired to do a job that I'm not willing to risk. Then there is that reckless side of my brain and it seems to be winning the argument I am having with myself. I swear my body is only connected to the reckless side because it is screaming at me to pull him back to me.

He leans over and his lips leave light kisses along my neck. "You have this pull on me, Cam, I'm done fighting it." His lips brush over my skin as he talks and that does it, my sensible side loses.

"Is this the best way to test this out? Straight to the hot and heavy part?" I make one last attempt at being smart and sensible.

"I know, I'm fighting the same thing right now. Tell me to go, Cam." He speaks in my ear and when he looks down at me his jaw does that flexing thing and I'm lost.

I may regret this in the morning. My hand goes to the back of his head and my fingers bury into the very short hair, my nails probably scraping a little too hard along his scalp. I come up to meet his lips. He moans and his lips slam against mine, his tongue instantly finding mine. He isn't going to give me another moment to think too much and stop him again because his hands are now both under my shirt and all thought of what a bad idea this is and how we are rushing way too fast have all vanished. That's all it takes. One touch, skin to skin, and I become one of those girls I told him I wouldn't be. He said that isn't what he was looking at this being but I'm definitely not playing hard to get right now either. His hand runs up and down my sides a couple of times like he is testing my reaction. I find the bottom of his shirt and run my hands up his back. I can feel the muscles flex as I lightly run my nails up and down. He works out, I can feel the evidence of it in every muscle in his back and the way they ripple under my touch.

He surprises me when he suddenly sits up next to me. The cool air touches my exposed skin and I have to hold back the whimper. He quickly pulls his shirt over his head and tosses it onto the floor. I hope I'm not drooling because his six-pack and perfect pecs are causing feelings in my body I have never felt before. My fingers itch to touch him.

My stomach is still exposed to him, Kade leans down and when his lips touch the skin above my belly button I about shoot off the bed. My back arches, begging him for more. My fingers dig more into his scalp. His hands on each side of my waist push my shirt up over my breasts and then ever so gently over my head. Even heated and in the moment of sexual tension he is aware of my injury and is careful not to hurt me. A tender side that I didn't think of Kade having until today, another thing making it hard to stay away from him.

My shirt gets tossed onto the floor somewhere, his hands come down over my shoulders and over my breasts. I've never been bothered by wearing a bra before, right now I want to beg that he tear it off as quickly as possible. The need to feel his hands on my naked breasts and massaging my nipples to hardened peaks is almost unbearable.

His lips touch the sensitive skin above my belly button again and start a trail up. His tongue lightly makes a trail between my breasts and then he kisses along my chest, up the side of my neck and finally his lips are back to mine, lightly this time.

Our eyes meet and I watch as his eyes search over the bruises on my face. "Maybe we shouldn't be doing this. I don't want to hurt you," he whispers.

"Kade, I'm fine, I promise to let you know if something hurts." He can't stop this now. I'm not against begging at this point.

Reaching behind my back, he unclasps my bra, pulling it down over my arms. The moment I feel flesh against flesh I'm done, he definitely isn't stopping now. I make a trail with my nails down his back, he closes his eyes and the deepest moan escapes from him. I smile up at him.

"Your smile is going to be my undoing, woman. I know I've been the reason why you haven't smiled much but I hope that changes."

"Kade, I want to feel all of you against me, please."

He smiles the sexiest smile I have ever seen. His lips claim mine and there is nothing gentle about it this time. His tongue finds mine, his hands mold around my breasts squeezing, his fingers pinching my nipples making them harder than they already were. I moan against his mouth, my back arches pushing my breasts into his hands. My fingers in his hair, I pull my lips away and guide his lips down to my chest. I can feel his smile against my skin. One hand goes to brace himself, the other squeezes my breasts as his tongue traces a circle around my nipple.

My hands work their way down his back, around his waist and to the front button of his jeans. I can feel the pressure of his hardness pressing at the front fly of his pants. Unbuttoning the button, I quickly slide the zipper down. His heaviness falls against my hand as the pressure of the zipper releases. I lightly stroke him, only the barrier of his boxer briefs between him and my hand.

His mouth sucks hard over my nipple and both of us moan. He pulls away from me and I whimper my disapproval of losing the heat over my now chilled nipple. Sitting up onto his knees, he makes quick work of my pants button and zipper, then pulls them down, panties and all, over my legs. He works his way off the end of the bed to finish stripping me of my remaining clothes and then I get to watch as he works his pants and remaining garments quickly down his legs. He bends down to remove his shoes and discard all clothing.

I would love to lie here and just enjoy the vision in front of me but I'm not given the chance. He joins me back on the bed, his knee between my legs. He leans forward and starts a row of kisses at my knee and slowly works his way upward. His lips touch the top of my inner thigh and I feel his hot breath on my now pulsing core and I hear myself whimper. I grab the pillow behind my head and hold on tight.

His tongue lightly runs up the most sensitive part of my body and I almost come undone right then. Closing my eyes, I grip the pillow tighter and bite down on my bottom lip. Everything rockets through my body the moment his tongue dips deep inside of me. I shoot up off the bed, my hands now in his hair pressing his face into me.

His hand comes up to my breast, he squeezes and I almost lose it right there. "Kade, I need you now, please."

He pulls away from me and I want to scream. The cold air that shoots around my flaming body right now almost causes me to lose myself.

Looking over at him, he is bent down grabbing something out of his pants. His wallet it looks like and then he tosses it back onto the floor without a care. I watch as he tears open the small little package and slips on the protection that I realize I didn't even think about. I'm on the pill, but I'm glad he is still in his right mind to think about it.

He joins me back on the bed, his lips claiming mine. I push my hand in between us and wrap my fingers around his very hard manhood. Sliding my hand down, I squeeze gently as I bring my hand up his full length.

"Cam, I need to be inside you." Kade speaks against my mouth as he presses himself harder into my hand.

His fingers are in my hair and as I stroke him once more they tighten, putting pressure on the injured side of my face. I bite my lip to keep from crying out, as much as it hurts I don't want him to end this. I must flinch because he pulls back.

"Damn it, Cammie, I'm so sorry. I told you this probably isn't a good idea right now."

I grab his arm with one hand. "Kade, I'm all right, please don't stop." With my other still around his hardness, I stroke him a couple of times.

Before I know it we are turned around and I am now straddling him, his hardness at my center begging to enter. I adjust slightly and sit fully down on him.

"Cam, you are so tight." Kade's hands go to my waist and he thrusts up, pushing himself deeper inside of me.

I place my hands behind me and brace myself on his thighs, this causes my body to take him in even deeper. My head falls back. When I look back at him, there is that wickedly sexy smile once again. He traces a hand down the valley between my breasts, over my stomach and then his fingers find that sensitive spot and I shoot up into a sitting position again. He sits up and his mouth goes straight to my nipple, his tongue and fingers working the same motion. My arms wrap around his shoulders and pushes his head tighter against me, my hips working against his hand.

I can't hold it back any longer, Kade bites down onto my nipple and I lose myself. My arms tighten around him, holding him to me. I can feel myself tighten around him, pulling him further inside of me.

Before I know what's happening, I'm under him once more, he has my hands above my head in his and he is thrusting hard into me as my body still comes apart around him. I'm not sure how much more I can take. With one last deep thrust, he moans, and I'm pretty sure I may scream a little, but everything sounds muffled in my ears to the pounding in my head and this isn't from the stitches. We lie still for a moment, just the sound of our breathing filling the room.

Slowly he pulls himself out of me and I'm not sure what I was expecting next but I know it wasn't for him to roll over to his side and pull me in tight against him. Nothing is said, I don't know what to say and part of me is waiting for him to get up, get dressed and leave, but he doesn't. His arms are tight around me and as time passes I can feel them loosen up a little, his breathing even outs and the biggest surprise of the night is Kade falling asleep holding on tight like he is afraid I will disappear while he's asleep.

CHAPTER TWELVE

KADE

I can hear the faint sound of something vibrating. Opening my eyes slowly, I see the light coming through the windows of the room. Cammie is still wrapped in my arms in the same position as when we fell asleep last night. We didn't move the entire night. There's the sound again, it's my phone going off in the pocket of my pants. I have no idea what time it is. Cammie starts to move next to me, and those small movements start waking up other parts of my body.

Again, the phone goes off. Damn!

"You better get up and answer that before they send out a search party." Cammie's sleepy voice sounds so damn sexy, I couldn't care less what they want. What I want right now is to be inside this woman again.

Her hand comes up and touches the bruised side of her head. I can see her eyes flinch a little, that instantly cools my need for her. She is hurting. Now I feel like a jerk for last night.

"Cam, are you all right?"

She nods against my arm.

"Cammie, turn around and look at me."

She tries to pull out of my arms and get up. "Kade, I'm fine."

Pulling her back down, I roll her over to her back and trap her under me. "You aren't all right."

She rolls her eyes. "I have a little headache, I'm fine."

She won't look me in the eyes. I'm not sure if that's because she doesn't want me to see the pain she's in or if it's that awkward morning after moment.

"Cam, look at me."

Still her eyes look everywhere other than at me. Leaning down I gently kiss her, when I pull back she has her eyes closed. I wait for her to open them, putting no space between us.

A small sigh escapes between her lips and her eyes open, looking directly into mine. She doesn't have a choice, I'm that close.

"Are you all right?" I ask once more.

"Your phone is going off again." She ignores my question.

"I don't give a damn about my phone, I need to know you are all right. Or are you regretting last night?"

She just stares up at me for a moment. Then surprises me when her hand goes to the back of my head and pulls me down the small distance between our lips, claiming mine this time.

"Then that's telling me you are hurting." I'm pretty sure this will be the only time I'm happy to know her head is hurting.

"I'm a little tender and have a small headache, but I can take some medicine and be fine."

Again, my phone vibrates. "Damn, what do they want?"

Reluctantly, I roll away from Cammie and search for my pants. Pulling my phone out of my pocket, I see Krystal's picture on the screen.

"What can I help you with?" I ask sarcastically.

"It's about time, we went to your room and knocked but no answer. Then the strangest thing, in the hallway outside of

Cammie's door, we found the dinner you were bringing up to her last night just laying there on the floor."

She is fishing for information and I'm not falling for the bait. "Krystal, what do you want?"

Cammie gets up, taking the sheet with her, wrapping it around her body. I watch as she grabs a couple of things out of her bag and then goes to the bathroom, shutting the door behind her.

"We are all meeting for breakfast and then getting on the road, Uncle Michael told me to call you," Krystal's voice comes through the phone reminding me she is there.

"All right."

The phone is silent for a moment, I think maybe she hung up but then again I should have known better.

"Do I need to go and get Cammie?" There is a knowing smile I can hear through the phone.

"I'm hanging up now, Krystal."

"All right, see you guys in a few minutes."

I hit end before she can say anything else.

Grabbing my pants, I pull them on and grab my shirt and shoes up off the floor. Walking over to the bathroom door, I knock. "Cammie, I'm going to head back to my room and change real quick, I'll be back and we can go down to breakfast."

"All right," is all of a response that I get back.

"Cammie, are you all right?" It is taking everything I have right now not to just open the door and check on her.

My hands are braced on each side of the door frame and I'm leaning forward trying to hear any sounds that aren't right through the door when it opens and Cammie is looking straight up at me.

"Kade, please don't take this the wrong way because I appreciate how attentive you have been since all of this has happened." She waves her hand over her bruises, which seem to look worse today than they did yesterday, "But Kade, you need to back down a little. I promise you that if something out of the ordinary starts to bother me or the pain is more than I can handle, I will say something to you. I'm going to experience some pain, I swear to you I am fine."

She is standing there in only a towel and looking sexy, it's driving me crazy not to have her again this morning, but I can't, she needs the rest and we need to get down with the others. However, I do need to taste her a little so I lean down and kiss her gently.

"I'm sorry, I'll back off a little," I smile down at her.

"Thank you, and don't think I didn't catch that 'little' part of what you just said. Go get dressed and I will meet you downstairs, all right?"

"Why can't we go down together, afraid of what everyone will say? I have a feeling no one is going to be surprised."

If Krystal already knows I stayed with Cammie last night I'm sure it's been the topic of conversation with everyone else this morning already.

"Cammie, I'm not going to hide us from everyone."

"I'm not saying we need to hide whatever may be happening between us, but the thing is it's new for you and me as well. I'd like us to figure it all out before everyone else decides to throw in their opinion."

"I'm pretty sure from the conversation I just had with Krystal everyone may know. Well, let's put it this way, Krystal knows I stayed here last night, so I'm sure everyone else will know the moment she meets up with all of them. She has a big mouth."

There are beads of water dripping down her shoulders and chest. My hands tighten around the door frame to keep from grabbing her and ripping that towel away from her and taking her back to bed.

"Kade, your dad may not be extremely happy about whatever this is that may be starting between us, and I happen to like my job."

"I don't give a damn what my dad has to say about what is starting between us, but I have a feeling he isn't going to be as upset as you may think. I'm not sure how you missed everyone's reactions yesterday but I didn't and there wasn't one person that looked like they were against you and me."

"I guess your caveman actions and carrying me to your truck was a little hard for everyone to miss." She smiles up at me and my knees about buckle.

I can't take the distance between us any longer. Wrapping an arm around her waist, I pull her body tight against mine.

"I can assure you no one is going to fire you, but I'm not going to walk around everyone like there isn't anything going on between us, Cam. One thing is for sure, though, if we don't agree on this soon I'm going to forget breakfast with everyone and will probably have to catch up with them on the road because I'm going to take you back to that bed and repeat last night. Then I can assure you that everyone is going to be talking."

"As tempting as that is, I'm going to be honest with you. I think my head is asking for a break." She touches the fresh bandage.

Kissing her lightly on the forehead, I step back. I knew this morning she was downplaying the pain she was in. "I'm going to go get changed real fast and grab my stuff. Then I'm going to meet you back here and we are going to go down to breakfast with every-one. All right?"

She looks hesitant for a moment but I recognize the moment she decides to give in, she takes a deep breath and nods. I still see the concern or maybe worry in her eyes and nothing I can say is going to take that away I'm realizing, I'm just going to have to show her it's all going to be all right.

IT TAKES me no more than fifteen minutes to take a fast shower and grab everything I brought up for the night. Knocking on her door, I'm more surprised that she answers than I would have been if she would have walked down before me.

"Are you ready to go?"

She already has her bag in hand and I reach out to take it from her. She doesn't hesitate to allow me to carry it for her.

"Thank you," she says and steps out of her room, shutting the door behind her.

The elevator doors close behind us and I notice her hands haven't stopped moving. In her pockets and then right back out. She plays with a fingernail and then shakes her hands like they fell asleep or something. Putting down our bags, I turn and grab her hands in mine. She looks up at me in surprise. Leaning down, I claim her lips, and her body instantly relaxes. I let go of her hands and they go right up into my hair. With one hand around her waist, I pull her in tight against me, my other goes into her hair and my tongue finds hers. A soft moan escapes from her and I try to remember why I fought this for the past few days.

The ding from the elevator alerts us that we are at the first floor and the doors open. Pulling back slightly from her, I ask, "Are you all right now?"

One moment she looks a little dazed the next she is stepping out of my arms and grabbing her own bag, walking out of the elevator in front of me. Grabbing my bag, I follow her out and in a couple strides I'm walking side by side with her.

"Should we hold hands?" I ask, smiling down at her.

Without missing a beat, she switches her bag to her hand that is next to mine and quickens her pace. This is one thing I like about her, she doesn't have to make a scene or want to be noticed and she isn't clingy. On the other side of it I find I want to take her bag from her hand and hold it to prove a point to her.

I know what she thinks my reputation is and she would be right. I have never been in a one-woman relationship. I started racing very early. When I was young it was all about riding, when

I hit the age of noticing girls it was all about playing and riding. I'm not going to deny I had my fun, but nothing serious. I wanted to concentrate on being number one, can't do that with a woman wanting all of your attention. A couple days ago when I met Cammie, something changed. Won't lie, it scares the hell out of me. Then that night she kissed me and I wanted to demand that Dad find someone else to do her job. I knew even then, I think, that I wasn't going to be able to stay away from this woman. I can't concentrate on being number one if I'm all caught up on a woman. The moment I knew for sure I was in trouble was when I found out how close Lucas and Cammie were. Lucas is one of my closest friends but the thought of him and Cammie knowing each other that well made me completely jealous. I've watched women fall at that man's feet, I think that's why we have so much fun when we go out together. How is it that Cammie and he have only been friends? I'm not a jealous man, I don't claim women and get possessive over them, but Cammie is different. I want to punch anyone who even looks at her like they may be interested in her.

As we walk up to the table, everyone else is already here and seated. There are only two seats left and they just happen to be next to each other. I hear Cammie's defeated sigh and I have to turn my head so that she doesn't see my smile. What's even better is that everyone continues on with their conversations as though we haven't even walked into the room, but if I look closer I can see that they are watching us without trying to be obvious about it.

My dad raises his hand up, getting the attention of the waitress, and she walks over. "Are you guys ready to order?" she asks.

"Yes, the party is all finally here now," my dad answers, looking at me.

I can feel Cammie's leg bouncing under the table. Placing my hand on her knee, she jumps a little. Glaring over at my dad, I warn him with my eyes that comments aren't needed or wanted.

He picks up on it and I see the little grin he isn't trying very hard to hide.

I squeeze her knee. Leaning over, I whisper to her, "Relax."

She surprises me when she grabs my hand. I'm expecting her to remove it from her leg but instead she squeezes it and keeps it tightly in hers.

CHAPTER THIRTEEN

CAMMIE

During breakfast I'm a little surprised no one makes a comment about Kade and me. I thought maybe at first Kade was wrong and no one knew. Though a closer look around the table, I catch the side looks we are getting. The one I watch the most is Michael. To my surprise I don't see any signs that he isn't approving of what may be happening between the two of us.

The rest of the drive to Vegas is uneventful. We make a couple of stops for gas, lunch, to just stretch our legs and to my relief Kade gives me space. He isn't always right next to my side, or holding my hand. I figured after this morning and the whole walking down together he would be wanting to prove his point. During the drive, he does reach over a couple of times and hold my hand and to my even more surprise Krystal doesn't make a big deal about it. Maybe I'm the one making too big of a deal about all of this.

We finally arrive in Vegas and everyone is ready to be out of the vehicles. Michael and Traci follow the rig over to the race location. They will be staying in the bus this weekend next to the rig. The rest of us are staying at one of the hotel casinos located on the Las Vegas Boulevard Strip.

Getting into the room, I unpack a few of my things, hanging up some stuff, and then lie down on the bed. It's quiet and relaxing to have a little alone time and I would love to get rid of the dull throb that is pounding my head right now. I haven't said anything to anyone because Kade would worry and start hovering over me.

It's all kind of strange really. That first day I met Kade or even the events that followed, I would never have guessed Kade would be the overprotective type, especially over a woman. With his family I expected it, I knew from the moment I watched him with his mom and Krystal how protective he was with them. Every time someone brings up his grandmother I can see the sadness in his eyes, I'll admit it makes him even more attractive to me. Any man who loves his grandmother that much can't be a total womanizer.

Five minutes, I'm sure that's all I've been lying here and someone is already at the door knocking. I'm starting to think this group never rests. I could ignore it but the last time I didn't answer my door Kade had the hotel staff opening it for him. Swinging my legs over the side of the bed, I stand up a little too fast, and the room spins a little. Whoever it is knocks again.

"I'm coming." If it is Kade I want him to know I'm all right and on my way.

Once the room settles again, I walk over and open the door to find Krystal.

"I couldn't wait any longer, the ride here was killing me. You have to tell me how this all happened. I've never seen my cousin like this." She is standing there bouncing on her toes like a little girl waiting to open a present or something. Here I thought no one was going to make a big deal about all of this.

I move to the side to let her in. "Come on in."

Krystal comes in and plops down in one of the chairs. "All right so spill it, what's going on between you and Kade?"

What makes you think anything is happening?"

Krystal rolls her eyes at me. "Please, I know he was with you this morning when I talked to him. I had gone to his room when he didn't answer my phone calls. I figured he had his phone on silent and wasn't hearing it so instead of telling Uncle Michael and having him get mad at Kade again for being irresponsible, I decided to go and try knocking. He didn't answer, when I looked down the hall I saw the bag from last night's dinner on the floor in front of your door. I put two and two together. I am still very curious on why your dinner was outside of your room."

Sitting down on the edge of my bed, I try to decide how much to tell her. Sam back at school was my best friend, but right now she is going through a lot and doesn't have a ton of time to talk and when we do talk it's all about Derrick, the man she is trying to convince herself that she doesn't need or want. It would be kind of nice to have another girlfriend to talk to and Krystal is very easy to talk to.

"Last night, I'm guessing when Kade was bringing up my dinner, he knocked and I had fallen asleep and didn't answer. Short version, he got worried, he called down to the front desk and had them come up and unlock my door. By the time I heard the knocks and got up to answer he was barging into the room. Would you believe me if I told you after that he was worried about me and wouldn't leave so he stayed the evening to watch me?"

From the look she is giving me she isn't buying any of that last part.

"Does it bother you? Kade and I?"

"There is only one thing that would have bothered me. I like you and I know how he is with women, I would be worried about him hurting you, but I have watched him with you the last couple of days and something has changed in him. I've waited for that one woman to come into his life and turn it upside down. He has been so sure that he wouldn't fall and I have a feeling he is falling and hard."

"I think you are overthinking everything a little."

"Look me in the eyes and tell me the only thing you two did last night was sleep. Cammie, you don't seem like the type of woman that needs to be taken care of. If he was wanting to stay just to watch over you last night then you are majorly downplaying this injury."

I could play that scenario, but then it would get back to Michael and he would be worried about me working. I'm not a good liar, never have been, I learned very young it just didn't work for me.

My silence is all Krystal needs to confirm what she already knows.

Taking a deep breath, I realize there is no reason to hide it. "I'll be honest, I'm very worried about his bad boy image. I met what he likes to surround himself with on the first day we met."

"All of his girls haven't been as bad as Brooke. None of us understand that situation. She won't be around for the longest time and then there she is again. I have no idea how she doesn't know how we all feel about her, no one hides their feelings about her."

"I don't think she cares what you guys think, she holds on tight to Kade. As long as the attention is there from him she couldn't care less. So you are saying this may be a bad idea?"

She is shaking her head no before the question is fully out of my mouth. "No, I think it's a great idea. I'm telling you, something has changed in him. Give him a chance."

She bounces up from the chair. "I came over to get the confirmation but also to tell you to get dressed, we are all going out tonight."

Normally I would jump right on that, I love going out, but I need this head to heal. "I appreciate the invite but I think I'm going to stay in tonight. I've been fighting a headache all day, I'm not going to be much fun." *Plus, there is no makeup that can hide the bruises on my face right now,* I think to myself.

I know she wants to argue with me, but she just nods. "All right, I understand, but if you change your mind we are heading out in about an hour."

"All right, if anything changes I'll definitely give you a call. You guys have fun, I'll see you in the morning." I walk her to the door, giving her a hug and shutting it behind her.

I'm kind of bummed, I want to be part of the group, go out and have a little fun. It's hard to keep from pulling the door back open and yelling down the hall at Krystal that I've changed my mind. Covering these bruises would be almost impossible and the slight throb in my head is reminding me that I need to take it easy.

Sitting down on the bed, the image of Kade out there tonight pops into my head. All the women hanging on him, it twists my stomach. Getting up, I walk over to my suitcase and pull out my cotton shorts and tank top. If I get comfortable then maybe I won't be so tempted to change my mind and go out with everyone. I have my laptop with me, I'll bring up a movie, that will keep my mind off what Kade is doing. I'll order dinner in and maybe I'll get some sleep tonight. I need to relax, let myself heal, and this is a good way to start. Listening to loud music, drinking and dancing is definitely not going to help. Why I think that if I was there Kade still wouldn't be having women all over him, I have no idea. We aren't in a relationship, we had sex once, there is nothing stopping him from hanging all over other women. The thought of watching that all night has me perfectly content hanging out in my room.

Looking into the bathroom, I see the spa-like bathtub. Now that looks very inviting. This group doesn't do anything cheap and right now I am very much appreciating it.

Sitting on the side of the tube I turn on the water, turning it as hot as my hand will allow me to. Quickly I pull off my boots and strip out of my clothes. Stepping over the ledge, I feel the hot water as my foot sinks into the tub. Now this was a very good idea. Sitting down, I lie back and let the tub fill up. Just as the water hits the jets that are all around the tub, I hit the button and it's heaven, the only word to use to describe it, pure heaven.

Sinking down, my whole body relaxes as the water flows over my shoulders and the back of my neck. I may just sleep in here tonight. Leaning my head back, I close my eyes. This is amazing! My stomach rumbles a little, maybe I should have ordered dinner first, but it's too late. Not getting out now, I smile to myself.

Ten minutes, I'm sure that's all I have had in heaven when someone decides to knock on my door. Moaning, I sink a little deeper into the water covering my ears. Maybe if I can't hear them they will just go away. Who would be here anyway? According to Krystal everyone is going out. Maybe whoever it is has the wrong room. If I don't answer they will go away.

Nothing else, good, maybe whoever it was decided to leave. There goes my ringtone now, are you kidding me? Taking a deep breath, I figure I better see who it is or I'm not going to get to enjoy this. Stepping out onto the soft rug, I grab the robe that is hanging on the back of the door. Tying the belt, I go to the door and look out the peep hole. Standing there is Kade, his phone up to his ear. Oh no, what if he is calling down to the front desk again?

Throwing open the door, I blurt, "I'm good, I'm here, don't send up someone to knock down the door."

"What took you so long to answer?" Kade is standing there in a dark pair of blue jeans and a black button-up shirt, the long sleeves rolled up, his hair messily styled and I want to run my hands through it.

Looking up at him, I arch my eyebrow in a questioning look. "Kade, I already told Krystal I wasn't going out with you guys tonight." I completely ignore his question.

Seeing him look as good as he does now and knowing he is out there isn't going to make relaxing very easy, I don't care how good that bathtub feels.

"I know, she told me, are you not feeling good?" He steps into the room and shuts the door behind him.

Him being this close, I get hit with how good he smells as well. "Kade, I'm fine, I just need to relax a little if I'm ever going to heal. Going out to loud music, drinking and dancing probably isn't going to set well later. I'm fine, I promise, you guys go and have fun."

His arm goes around my waist and pulls me in tight against him. "I'm not going out without you, Cam. You should have called me, we could have grabbed something to eat and then came back up and watched a movie or something."

"I don't want to hold you back from having fun, Kade, I promise you I'm good. I'm going to order some dinner and have it brought up and watch a movie on my laptop, probably knock out early." I keep my arms at my sides. I know the moment I wrap myself around him, smelling and looking as good as he does right now, I will be begging him to pick staying with me.

Stepping back, he takes my hand and leads me back into the bathroom. Once inside, he turns back to me, his hands going to the belt of my robe. Pulling the belt, it unties from around my waist and the robe falls open. He pushes it down my arms and I let it fall to the floor.

"Get back in the tub." He stands there and waits.

I turn and step in the tub, sinking back down into the hot water. This time it's not relaxing at all. Visions of him with women hanging all over him are bouncing around in my head. When he turns and walks out of the room my heart sinks, this is going to be the longest night.

My head falls back against the tub, shutting my eyes I take a couple deep breaths. I keep repeating to myself that I need to stay right where I'm at.

I hear his voice in the other room, it's low so I can't make out what he is saying or who he could be talking to. I wait a couple of minutes, waiting for him to come back in and tell me he is leaving or hear the door. I just need to relax, I can't worry about it, I shouldn't be worried about it.

Again laying my head back, I close my eyes and take a deep breath, I can't change things. Hearing his footsteps, I open my eyes as he walks back into the bathroom.

"I ordered some dinner. It should be here in an hour. I hope you like burgers."

I'm about to say thank you but am stopped as I watch as he starts to unbutton his shirt. It falls to the floor and he starts on the button of his pants. That's when I noticed he isn't wearing any shoes or socks.

"What are you doing, Kade?" My insides tingle and my core heats up just watching as he strips down in front of me.

"Sit up," he orders as he steps into the bathtub with me.

I don't even question him, I just do as he says. He slides down behind me, his arm hooks around my waist and he pulls me back between his legs and up against his chest.

"We have an hour before dinner arrives, I figured you would want a little time to relax before we ate and I wasn't going to pass up an opportunity to have your naked wet body pressed up against mine." He kisses me behind the ear.

My head falls back against his shoulder. "Kade, you don't have to stay here with me."

"I was only going out tonight because I wanted to be with you. If you are staying here, I'm staying here. Cam, if I went and you were here, I would sit there the whole time wondering if you are all right. I'd much rather be where I'm at right this moment." He trails kisses down my neck to my shoulder.

I moan and my head falls to the side, giving him better access. "No moaning, Cam. I am trying to behave here. I'm going to hold you for a little while then we are going to get out and have our dinner and then lie back and watch a movie, that's it."

"What if I want more?" I ask in a whisper.

"As hard as this is for me, because to be inside of you again would be amazing, I've thought of nothing else since last night, you need to rest and heal so that way the next time I'm inside of you I don't have to hold back." His breath tickles my neck.

Last night was holding back? My core throbs with this new information and I want to beg him to show me what not holding back is like. I thought last night was amazing.

"I'm fine, Kade, don't make me beg because right now I'm very close to begging."

"Cam, you were hurting last night and you are staying in tonight. We are going to have to hold out for tonight. I'm all right with just holding you."

All right with just holding me? Those are words I never expected to hear from Kade. Each day I'm learning something new about him and it's making it harder and harder to not fall for this guy. It would be so much easier to ignore this thing between us if he was the player I believed him to be.

Taking a deep breath, I try to calm the fire that's burning inside right now. Again my head lays back against his shoulder and I close my eyes.

"That's it, Cam, just relax."

AS MUCH AS I want him, after a little while that need calms, never disappearing altogether, but it isn't an ache any longer. I will even admit it is very relaxing. I find myself a little disappointed when there is a knock at the door.

"That's our dinner."

"Do you think eating is really necessary right now?" I have absolutely no desire to move, I don't care how wrinkled my body must be right now, I can't remember ever being this relaxed. That dull throb I've had all day is gone now.

"As much as I like having your wet, naked body pressed against mine, I'm starving." He kisses my cheek and then sits me up and away from him.

I watch as he steps out of the tub and grabs the robe I was wearing earlier. "I'm hungry, too, but you are denying me the nutrients that I'm wanting right now." I look up and give what I'm hoping is a very sexy smile.

He kneels down next to the tub and claims my lips, it's a hungry kiss and all I want to do is wrap my arms around him and pull him back into the water.

"Trust me, Cam, this is not easy for me either. Tasting you, being deep inside of you, hearing you moan in pleasure, sounds delicious right now, but I can't, I'm sorry. It kills me knowing you are in pain, I need you better, then I promise you won't have to beg. I will have no problem taking you whenever and wherever you want me to."

"Kade, talking like that isn't making things any easier here." I'm breathless and the heat that is boiling deep in my center is going to explode just from his words.

Whoever is at the door knocks again. "Get out and get dressed, I'm going to get our dinner and then I'm going to run back to my room and grab some sweats and I'll be right back. Pick a movie for us."

He stands up and leaves the bathroom before I can say anything else, shutting the door behind him. I completely understand the whole needing a cold shower thing right now. I look over to the shower and contemplate jumping in real fast and cooling down.

HEARING the faint sound of an alarm clock, I stir slightly. I can't move much, I'm being held in place by Kade's arm draped around me, his leg over mine, his chest pressed tightly against my back.

"Ignore it," his deep, groggy voice whispers in my ear.

"Don't we need to be at the track by eight?"

"I'm thinking five more minutes won't hurt." His breath tickles my ear.

"Can you at least turn it off, hit snooze, something?" The alarm gets a little louder with every thirty seconds he lets it go off.

"I would have to move to do that and right now I don't want to move."

Turning my head, I try to give him a glare over my shoulder but I can't move my head much. His lips touch my cheek. "We can't be late, Kade."

"How are you feeling this morning? Should you skip today and rest before things get really crazy this weekend? Today is only registration and trial runs, tomorrow is when all the excitement happens. I'm sure my dad will understand if you need one more day to rest."

"Kade, I'm fine, no headache this morning at all. I'm here to do a job and I'm going to do it. I'm tougher than you seem to be making me out to be." I try to pull away from him and out of his arms but he just tightens himself around me.

"I'm sorry, that's not what I meant."

"Can you please turn the phone off?" I'm starting to get frustrated, at him and the damn phone alarm.

He untangles himself from around me and reaches over and shuts the alarm off.

"Thank you, now get up. If we are even a minute late your cousin will be knocking at my door. I'm sure they already know where you are since you didn't go with them last night."

Kade scoots himself over to me, wrapping his arm around my waist. "That's a bad thing?"

I know everyone already knows something is going on between Kade and myself but I'm still trying to be professional about it.

"Kade, this is your family and friends, I'm one of the employees. I don't want them thinking I'm not being serious about my job."

"So you think they are thinking you aren't professional because you are with me." There is amusement in his voice, he is laughing at me.

I don't want to do this with him right now. I try to get up from the bed but his arm tightens around my waist. "Kade, I need to jump in the shower before we go."

He lets go of me and jumps up off the bed, then holds his hand out to me. "That sounds like a great idea."

I stand without taking his hand and walk over to my suitcase. "I think you need to go back to your room and get ready. I'll meet you over there when I'm ready to go."

"Cam, I'm not hiding us, there is no reason for it."

"I'm not asking you to hide us. I'm asking that you go and get ready in your room so that I can get ready in mine."

Turning around I have to take a deep breath. He is standing there in only a pair of sweatpants that are sitting low on his hips. My hands itch to reach out and run them over his bare chest. When I look up he has that damn sexy smile of his.

"Are you sure you don't want me to join you in the shower?" He takes a step toward me.

I place my hand onto his chest to stop him. Wrong move. My nails dig into his skin and I take a deep breath, trying to calm my rapid heart. His hand goes to the back of my neck and he pulls me in, sealing his lips over mine. His tongue instantly finds mine and I'm pretty sure the moan I hear comes from me. The clothes I was holding in my other hand fall to the floor and my hand sinks into his hair at the back of his neck. I don't even realize that he has backed us into the bathroom until my back-side hits the counter. His hands make quick work of removing my shirt and shorts and my hands push down his sweatpants and boxer briefs. He turns me around so that I'm facing away from him, but can clearly see him behind me through the mirror. Kade trails kisses down my neck, his hands come around and cup both my breasts, squeezing them together. My head falls back against his shoulder but I keep my eyes on his through the mirror.

"I'm trying to stay away from you so you can heal, but I'm finding it harder and harder, all I want is to be inside you. Having you once is definitely not enough." His breath is warm against my cheek.

"If you stop now it will hurt me more than having you. Please, Kade, don't stop."

One of his hands travels down from my breast, over my stomach and I watch as his fingers disappear between my legs. The first touch against my wet core is almost all I can take. I want him so bad that just a touch almost has me losing it all together. I close my eyes when his fingers push deep inside of me.

"Don't hide your eyes from me, Cam, open them so I can watch them change as I bring you to your release."

Between the rhythm of his fingers and the words he's whispering in my ear, I'm not sure how much longer I can hold out.

"Kade, please." There is no shame in begging, not with this man.

He pulls his fingers from me and I almost scream in protest. He turns me back around to him and effortlessly picks me up. I find myself wrapping my legs around his waist, I can now feel his hardness against my wet center. As he walks backwards he rubs up against my core and my breath hitches. He sits down onto the edge of the tub, me sitting on his lap, my legs wrapped around his waist. His hand goes between us and he guides himself into me. I sit down as far as I can, feeling him deep inside of me.

"I'm at your mercy, Cam. Your pace, your pleasure, but I want your eyes at all times."

His hands are on my hips and I gently begin to rock, with each thrust of my hips into his I can feel him deeper and deeper. My head falls back.

"No, Cam, eyes on me."

I bring my head back up and he smiles, his eyes are turning different shades of green as I stare into them. He says I'm in control but his hands on my hips are urging me faster. My hands on his shoulders, my nails dig into his skin as my body shakes. My forehead goes down onto his, our eyes only inches apart, watching the desire roll around in his eyes makes my release more intense.

"Kade." His name is hissed between my teeth as I bite down onto my bottom lip, trying to hold back from screaming.

I've never held eye contact before like this and the intensity is so much greater as I watch Kade's eyes turn from white, almost pale green to a bright emerald green when he finally lets go of his release. His lips are instantly on mine, hard, as we both come down from the sexual high we have both just experienced.

A person's eyes will tell you anything if you pay close enough attention and in this moment I realized Kade is just affected by me as I am him.

CHAPTER FOURTEEN

KADE

I knew something was going to be different with Cammie, that's why I tried to fight the pull I kept feeling every time we were in the same space as each other. That first kiss was when I knew for sure I no longer wanted to be the player, I wanted to be the man that deserved her. I still fought it, though. I need to concentrate on one thing and that's winning this season, but now with her in my arms while I'm still deep inside of her, I have no idea why I wanted to keep my distance.

Last night I lay there in bed with her watching a movie. She only made it through maybe thirty minutes before I heard her breathing change to a relaxed tempo. She was curled up against my side with the softest little snore coming from her. I've never just lay in bed and held a woman. I've never just held a woman period anywhere. We have our fun and then the night is over, sleepovers are way too personal. Brooke is the only woman I can think of that I have been with more than once, maybe twice and she never said anything about our arrangement. One of the reasons I always fell back to her is she never pushed.

Something twisted inside when I watched Cammie as she

came apart in my arms just now. Her eyes shined to the brightest blue color, then as she was taken over by her release they turned smoky but they pierced me like they were seeing right through me. It was the most personal and private experience I've ever had with a woman.

"Your phone is ringing." Her lips move against mine.

"I really don't care about my phone or whoever may be calling me right now." That damn phone seems to have the worst timing.

She laughs and I have to hold my breath, I'm still inside of her and her laughing just ignites a need for her in me again.

"Kade, I already told you I don't want to be late." She tries to scoot off my lap but I hold her right where she is, I'm not ready to move.

"Are you complaining about the way I have taken up your time?"

She leans forward and gently kisses my lips. "I'm not complaining, but I'm also saying I don't want to be late."

Her hands on my shoulders, she slowly starts pulling back away from me. She must still be a little sensitive because she moans as I'm being pulled out of her.

"Don't make those noises, Cam, or we aren't going to be leaving this room anytime soon."

That makes her move a little faster, she is up off my lap and taking a couple steps back before I can stop her.

"Go and check your phone, I need to grab a fast shower."

"It would help if we just jump in together, we would get out of here faster."

"No, I'm going to take a shower alone, you are going to go and answer your phone that is once again going off and then going back to your room and getting ready to go so that everyone isn't waiting for us." She grabs a towel and wraps it around her body. I watch as she reaches in and turns the water on and stands there looking at me like she is waiting for me to leave.

Getting up, I walk over to her and lightly kiss her. "Fine, I will go and get ready on my own. Be ready in twenty minutes and I'll come by and grab you so we can head out."

"Thank you, I'll be ready." She smiles as she drops the towel and steps into the shower.

It takes everything in me not to say screw it and follow her in, but she is so worried about what everyone, especially my father, will think I don't want to push her. Grabbing my sweats up from the floor, I quickly put them on and walk out of the bathroom. My shirt is on the chair where I left it last night, I've never been able to sleep with one on. My phone goes off and it's my father.

"Good morning, Dad."

"Kade, why haven't you answered you phone?"

"In the bathroom, Dad, what's up?" Wasn't a lie, I was definitely in the bathroom!

"Krystal was trying to get ahold of you to find out when you guys were leaving. When she couldn't get ahold of you she called me. Just want to make sure you aren't running late."

Rolling my eyes, I take a deep breath. "I'll text her now, we should all be ready to go in about twenty minutes. I'll call you when we get there."

"All right, I already have your name and info at the gate for you, you shouldn't have any problem getting in the area."

"Sounds good, see you in a bit."

I don't wait for him to respond, I hang up my phone and head out of Cammie's room and back to mine, sending Krystal a quick text as I walk down the hall.

PULLING UP, I park between the bus and the rig. The place is already buzzing, riders and crews everywhere getting ready for the weekend.

"We have to get you both over to registration." Dad steps out of the bus the moment we pull in.

He is in manager mode and it is all business. No hi, how's your morning, it's let's get things done and get you boys on the track.

"I have the schedule for today, the sighting lap will be starting in a couple hours."

"What's a sighting lap?" Cammie leans over and whispers to me.

"We get to make a lap around the track to inspect it. Kind of familiarize ourselves with it."

"Boys, go get changed. Cammie, why don't you go in and check out the room. We moved things around and added some cargo type netting up on the shelves, there should be no flying boxes."

Everyone laughs, I don't. "Not funny, guys."

Cammie elbows me in the side. "Lighten up, it was a little funny."

"Having your head split open and a concussion isn't something I find to be funny."

She is no longer wearing the bandages over the stitches and even though it looks like the bruising may be starting to lighten up a little, it still looks bad. Leaning over, I lightly kiss her forehead. Pulling back, I notice her eyes looking in my dad's direction and her cheeks seem to have brightened a little.

When I look in his direction he gives me a slight nod of approval and is smiling. I've been trying to tell her my father wouldn't have a problem but maybe now she will believe me.

"Come on, Cammie, I'll go in with you and help, save you if anything decides to jump out at you." Krystal takes her by the hand and pulls her toward the rig side door.

"Not funny, Krystal!" I shout after them.

"Lighten up, Kade!" she yells back over her shoulder and then they disappear through the door.

Cody follows the ladies but doesn't say a word. There is at least one smart one in that relationship.

I take a step toward the rig to get changed. "Kade, wait up for a minute," Dad stops me.

"What's up?"

"Listen, your mom and I have no problem with what's going on between you and Cammie. We both saw this happening from the moment you two met, it was written all over both of your faces that you were attracted to each other. I want you to remember this, though. It cannot come between your racing and her job."

I catch myself before I roll my eyes at my father. I get where he is coming from, we have all worked hard to get to this point and I plan on being number one this season. I've had this conversation with myself more than a couple of times but I couldn't stay away, I just need to make it all work out.

"Kade, I'm not going to sit here and lecture you on what is important, I know you know all of that. Remember, though, this isn't just your job this could affect."

"Dad, trust me, I have thought about all of this but I couldn't seem to talk myself away from her, I tried. I finally figured it would be better to work with it than against it."

"Just remember she isn't one of the girls like Brooke."

Now I roll my eyes. "Dad, please, I'm aware of the type of woman Cammie is. I'm not looking for the one-night thing with her, she is different, and I'm different around her. I can't sit here and promise that everything is going to work out between the two of us, who can predict that?"

"Listen, your mom asked me to talk to you. I have, that's the last you will hear from me about this. Now go and get ready, we need to get you two registered." He turns and walks back to the bus without another word.

Heading to the rig to get changed, I run into Krystal as she is coming back out. "All is safe, no flying boxes." She pats me on the shoulder as she moves around me.

"It's a good thing I love you."

"You need to loosen up, smile a little more. She isn't fragile, but if you smother her she isn't going to stay around."

I know Krystal is right. I have this intense need to protect Cammie even though I know she doesn't need my protection.

"I get it. I'm working on it. Now let me go get ready."

"I love you and I like her, just don't want you messing it up." She gives me a kiss on the cheek and then moves past me and over to the bus.

I start up the stairs once again, only this time to run into Cammie. "Everything all good?" I back down the stairs so that she can come down.

"Yes, everything looks good. Cody wants me to work out his shoulders a little before the practice laps, so I'm going to go and ask your dad for the schedule. Is there anything you need stretched before you get started?"

I have to hold off the comment I want to make over what I need worked out, she is in professional mode and we need to keep it professional right now, we have plenty of time for play. I want her to know I'm taking her seriously and that this thing that is forming between the two of us isn't going to cause a problem in the work place.

"Actually, I should probably have you work the knee a little."

"No problem." She places her hand against my chest and places a soft kiss on my lips.

I push my hands into my pockets to keep from grabbing her around the waist and pulling her tight to me and claim her lips in a kiss promising what is to come later tonight.

"I'm going to go get changed, you go get the schedule. I'll see you in a bit." I place a quick kiss on her forehead and quickly move around her and up the stairs before I lose all restraint.

CHAPTER FIFTEEN

CAMMIE

If someone would have asked me a year ago, or even a month ago, if I would like to go to a motocross race, I probably would have given them an "are you kidding" look. This may be why Lucas never brought it up that he was into the sport, he knew how I would react. I'm a country girl. I like rodeos, guys in jeans that fit nicely over their butts. Horses, bulls, cowboy boots.

Motocross is nothing like I expected it to be. It's not the eight seconds of excitement that you get with bull riding, and I would think after about two laps I'd get bored with watching, but my eyes never leave Kade as he circles around the course. I find myself holding my breath more than a few times when another rider tries to get around him and I watch their tires become only inches apart from each other as they battle for the spot. A bull is strong. A rider needs to hold on for eight seconds and try to control the beast they are sitting on while the clock winds down. In motocross, I watch as each rider has to control the bike they are riding, through jumps and turns, over numerous sections of what someone told me is called the whoops section of the track. Watching their arms pump up and down with the handle bars as the tires ram into the ground, the riders' knees absorbing each of the landings. A rider needs to be in top shape to keep this up for a full race which I find out lasts about thirty minutes. At some of these series they may have to ride multiple times a day.

I have watched a couple of collisions. The rider goes down and it's all by chance that another rider doesn't run into them while they are down. Kind of like a bull charging a rider once the rider has been bucked off or jumps off after their eight seconds. The two sports aren't really all that different.

Yesterday I was a little bored. The day consisted of registration, practice laps and the sight laps. It wasn't a very exciting day and I wondered how anyone could find the sport exciting. On our way back to the hotel for the evening, both Cody and Kade asked if I was hooked yet. I've never been a good liar so I just responded with a shrug of my shoulders and told them to ask me when the weekend was over, hoping it became a little more exciting.

Today is a completely different. The atmosphere all around is different. Even Kade has been in a different mood. He's more serious, kind of quiet. Only riders and the mechanics get passes to be on the track and Krystal is off doing what she does best, photography. I find a spot where I can stand and watch the boys race. There is a gentleman who stands next to me that answers my endless amount of questions.

Cody is a different class of rider than Kade so I watch him first and I'm impressed, by the time Kade's race is over I find that I'm completely hooked.

I work out Cody's arms and legs while Kade is finishing up with what needs to be done when a race is over. I guess after a win, the bike gets taken for inspection, for what I'm not sure. Both guys took first today and will each run one more race tomorrow.

Cody is done and going for a shower and to change. I start getting ready for Kade to get back, I'm sure he is needing to be rubbed out as well. I'm smoothing out the sheet over the table when the door opens.

"Congrats, babe, you did great." I wrap my arms around his neck and try to give him a kiss but he pulls back.

He doesn't say anything, he just stands there. His hands are at my waist but instead of pulling me into him he is pushing me away. My arms drop and I step out of his grasp. "Are you all right?"

"My knee is flaring up." He doesn't look at me, he just sits himself up onto the table.

He has already changed out of his riding pants, now only wearing a pair of spandex type bicycle shorts. I'm assuming it's what he wears under his pants while he is riding.

I'm trying not to take his mood personally. I would think after winning a race a person would be excited. Cody was exhausted but he was in a good mood and talked to me.

Walking around the table, I stop in front of him and work my hands around his knee. "It feels a little swollen, how did it feel during the race?"

"About halfway through it started to throb a little." His answer is very monotone and he isn't looking at me.

"Did anything pop that you felt?"

He just shakes his head. I notice his hands are gripping the side of the table. His grip is pretty tight, his knuckles are white. Maybe he is in more pain than he is telling me.

I press around on the sides and watch his facial expressions as I do, but they never change.

"Kade, I can't fix this if you aren't going to tell me what you are feeling. If it hurts you need to let me know where so that I know what to concentrate on."

Instead of answering me he hops down off the table. The space in the room is very limited, we are now chest to chest, but not for long. He steps to the side and opens the door to leave.

"It will be fine, I'll just take a couple aspirins." Before I can respond he is out of the room, closing the door behind him.

What on earth just happened? I'm trying to convince myself that he is just tired, but something is telling me there is a lot more to this than him just being tired.

I'm not playing the game, though. If he doesn't want to talk to me and he wants to limp around on an injured knee then he can. When he wants to talk, he knows where I am.

Cleaning up the room real quick, I get it set back up and ready for tomorrow and with nothing else to do I head out of the rig.

There is no one around. I see movement through the windows of the bus but I'm not sure who it is. There is a picnic table set up under the awning of the bus so I decide to wait there until everyone is ready to go.

Cody and Krystal come out of the bus about fifteen minutes later.

"Cammie, what are you doing out here? Why didn't you come in?" Krystal comes over and sits next to me.

Shrugging my shoulders, I put my phone back in my pocket. "I'm good, still kind of new at all of this so not really sure what happens and when. I didn't see anyone so I figured I'd just sit here and wait, it's no big deal."

"Where is Kade?" Cody asks, looking around.

I want to tell them that he is probably pouting somewhere, but instead I just shrug my shoulders again.

Then as though he knew he was being talked about, he comes out of the trailer. He steps down the stairs and walks over in our direction. I watch his steps and notice he is favoring his injured knee. Serves him right, maybe he should get over himself and allow me to help him.

"Are we ready to head back?" He looks at Cody and then Krystal, but not me.

"What's the plan for dinner tonight?" Krystal asks all of us.

"Honestly, I'm thinking we just grab something either on the way or maybe just at the hotel then call it a night. I'm exhausted and have an early race in the morning," Cody goes on to explain.

I have to say I'm a little surprised. It's Saturday night and we are in Vegas, I expected they were going to want to go out tonight. I'm a little relieved that's not the case.

"I think I'm just going to have something sent up to my room and call it a day," Kade pipes in.

I notice the look Krystal gives him and then me. She thinks he just wants to get me alone, but her smile fades as she looks between us. Her eyes meet mine and I can see the question in them. I shake my head at her and shrug my shoulders, letting her know without words that I have no idea what his problem is. I'm relieved when she doesn't question him.

"All right. Well, Cammie, they have a great steakhouse back at the hotel, I was thinking that sounded good for dinner. Do you want to join Cody and I?"

I look over at Kade, he isn't looking directly at me but he is listening to our conversation. I can tell by the way his head is slightly tilted toward us. I'm not going to play games with him, we are two grown adults and I have no interest in a relationship with anyone who can't act like an adult.

"I'm in, steak actually sounds pretty good." Getting up, I start for the truck. I have no idea what I did to be getting this kind of reaction from Kade but I'm done with the game. I have no problem going back to the hotel, having a great dinner with friends then turning in for the night with a movie alone in my room. It actually sounds like a great plan. Kade can spend the evening alone in his room.

THE RIDE back to the hotel is a quiet one. I look back once and see that Cody is already asleep, and Krystal is flipping through pictures that she had taken of the guys on her camera. I just stare out the passenger side window and watch Vegas as we pass through it.

A couple of times Krystal passes her camera over to me to show me a shot she took. I'm impressed with her talent.

"Cammie, you have to check out this picture of Kade." Krystal once again passes the camera over the back of my seat.

The screen on the back of her camera isn't very big so it amazes me at what I'm looking at. Kade is coming around one of the corners and dirt is flying up behind him, but what catches my attention the most about the pictures is his eyes. Even with his goggles on and this tiny screen, I can see the intensity in his green eyes. The concentration, yet a small spark of cockiness as he knows he is in first place and will stay there. They are almost smiling, but so concentrated.

"Krystal, your talent behind that camera is something else. This is a great picture. When you get a chance, can you send me this one?"

I pass the camera back to her. Looking in Kade's direction, I notice that muscle in his jaw flex and I find myself fighting the need to reach over and wrap my hand around the back of his neck and bury my fingers into his hair, silently showing him what I would like to do with him once we were alone, but instead I lock my hands within each other and turn my attention back out the passenger side window.

"Sure, I'll probably download them all on the drive back home, it will give me something to do. I'll get it over to you then."

"Thank you."

The rest of the drive to the hotel is quiet, well, with the exception of Cody snoring in the back seat.

. . .

CODY, Krystal and I decide to go straight over and grab dinner when we get back to the hotel. I watch Kade as he splits away from us and heads to the elevators as we head in the direction of the restaurant.

"What is Kade's problem?" Krystal asks once he is gone and heading in the opposite direction.

"I wish I knew. He came in to get his knee worked on after the race but he was short with me and wouldn't look me in the eye. I didn't even touch him before he got up and walked out of the room. I was going to ask you if this was normal behavior after a race."

Krystal just shakes her head no.

We are just sitting down when my phone goes off with a text. Pulling it out of my pocket, I see that it's from Kade.

Kade: I need you to come by my room.

I roll my eyes.

Me: Why?

I pick up my menu and look through it while I wait for his response, coming across the drinks section of the menu first. Yes, a drink sounds great right now.

Kade: We need to talk

Oh now he wants to talk! I think to myself.

Me: I already tried talking to you and you decided to walk out of the room. By the way, how is that knee doing?

I wish I could figure out how to text with sarcasm, because I know exactly how that knee is, I've watched him limp around on it since.

Kade: Why are you being so stubborn?

Is he kidding right now?

Me: I'm pretty sure I'm not the stubborn one today. I think we need to call it a night. After I eat I'm going to my room, turning on a movie and probably falling asleep at the beginning of it. I'll see you in the morning.

I'm not doing this with him right now. I turn the volume down on my phone and shove it back into my pocket. This conversation can wait until after dinner, or maybe tomorrow, I don't need him ruining my time with people who would like to be around me at the moment.

"Is everything all right?" Krystal asks over her menu.

I nod my head. "Yep, everything is great. I do have one question for you, though. Is Kade the jealous type when he has a girlfriend?"

"Honestly, that I know of, Kade really hasn't had a steady girlfriend. The only person I have seen him with more than once is Brooke and I know there isn't really anything serious there, I think that's more convenience than anything."

My phone vibrates in my pocket a couple of times, I know they are from Kade, but I'm ignoring them. I pick up my menu and decide to enjoy my dinner.

THE REST of dinner my phone goes off a couple of times, but other than that it is nice to sit and talk with Cody and Krystal. They answer a couple of the questions I have about racing and things that happened today. I'm finding that I am quickly becoming addicted to this sport.

We talk for a couple of hours down at the restaurant, have a couple of beers and then decide to head back up to the rooms. We have an early morning for the final race day and Cody looks exhausted.

I grab a quick shower and even decide to order a brownie/ice cream dessert that is pictured on the brochure next to my bed and have it delivered up to me.

When the knock comes to the door, I don't even bother to look out the peep hole to see who it is, I just assume it's my dessert.

Opening the door, I'm greeted by a very pissed off Kade and not my delicious dessert I've been looking forward to.

"Why aren't you answering my texts?"

All right, enough, I can't do this. I don't even invite him in. "I was having dinner and your texts were putting me in a bad mood."

"You almost cost me the race today."

I know I must be looking at him like he has grown a second head or something. I have no words to even respond to him on that one. Did he really just say that I almost cost him the race today? I think back to the race. There was one moment when another rider almost overtook him on one of the curves after they ran side by side on the whoops, but Kade outmaneuvered the rider and held his spot like the pro he is.

"Would you care to explain?" I finally find my voice.

"Did you think because I was riding, I wouldn't see you flirting with other guys?"

The only guy I even talked to was the older gentleman who was standing next to me. Who was being nice enough to answer the million questions I was firing off as I was watching Kade ride. I think back to the race and after. I remember watching Kade and Michael having a conversation after the race, I couldn't hear what was being said. Kade looked a little irritated with his father as they spoke but I honestly didn't take it as a bad conversation, however if his dad was lecturing him over the spot when that rider almost passed him that could be a bad thing. On the flip side of it, I'm not going to be his excuse for him every time he has a bad race.

The hotel employee shows up next to Kade with a tray in his hands. I take the slip from him, signing for my dessert, adding the tip on it for him and then take the tray from him. Thanking him, I set the tray on the table next to the door. I'm not going to walk away and chance Kade following me into my room, I need to keep him in the hallway and away from my bed.

If Kade thinks I'm going to become a reason for his bad day, he is mistaken. That won't lead to anything good and will most likely change Michael's opinion on us even being in a relationship at all. I won't have this affecting my job or Kade's.

"The older gentleman you are referring to was only answering the load of questions I was asking during your race. I was fascinated with watching you. The man you are referring to was probably old enough to be my father, but that aside even if he wasn't, you have absolutely no reason to blame me for a mistake on your part. Kade, I will not be the person or reason you use every time something goes wrong on the track. So with that said and as much as I really don't want to end what has started between us like this, I'm thinking it's better if we just end whatever has started. You have a lot riding on this season and I'm not going to be the fall guy in this relationship. I love this job, and I won't do anything to chance losing it."

"I'm not letting you walk away from us, Cam." His arms are spread apart above his head, his hands braced on the door frame.

"You don't really have a choice, Kade. We both have a job to do and we both need to put our concentration on that right now."

He just stands there, his head bent down, but that muscle in his jaw is flexing. My hand tightens around the door handle to keep from reaching out and pulling him into me and kissing him. This isn't going to be easy, but I'm not going to be the excuse he uses.

"Goodnight, Kade." I shut the door before I do something that will probably be amazing but completely wrong.

Placing my forehead against the door for a moment, I wait. I don't hear anything from the other side. Looking up into the peep hole, I find that he is no longer standing there. Disappointment floods through me, it would have been nice if he would have fought a little more, but this just confirms to me that I'm right by breaking this off now. My chest tightens and the tears well up in my eyes, he just isn't ready!

I lift the lid from the tray which contains my dessert. The ice cream has already started to melt and it no longer looks as mouth-watering as it did thirty minutes ago. I set the lid back down and leave it sitting on the table next to the door.

Sitting on the bed, I stare at the black screen of the television. A movie isn't sounding good either, so instead I turn out the lights and lie down, pulling a pillow in tight against me. A couple tears fall down my cheeks and I promise this is all the time I'm going to allow myself to be heartbroken. I've been hired on to do a job and I'm going to do it, while Kade focuses on winning this season.

CHAPTER SIXTEEN

KADE

I can't go back to my room and I can't knock down Cammie's door and make her change her mind about the two of us, so I end up at the bar instead. I shouldn't be here, I have a race at eight in the morning. I should be wrapped around Cammie after an evening of indulging in her body for a couple of hours, sleeping.

No, I decide to go and accuse her of flirting with someone and then blame her for being the reason I almost came in second today. What the hell is wrong with me? I'm not the possessive type, well, at least I didn't think I would be. I could go up and apologize to her, but something tells me that isn't going to help very much tonight.

Maybe she is right, maybe the timing is completely off for the two of us. Today is proof of that. I was distracted by her today on the track. Every time I passed the spot where she was standing my attention went to her and wondering what was going on. I wasn't paying attention to the track in front of me, the competition coming up behind me, or trying to pass me, I was only concentrating on her. I'm actually surprised I finished the race at all, let alone in first. My parents and this team are expecting me to take first this season, the team can always use the money and the sponsors it will bring. I need to make sure all my concentration is on that the next couple of months, not on a woman.

Downing the last of my beer and looking down at my watch, I realize I'm only going to get a couple hours of sleep tonight. There, another sign that maybe this is best. I can't have my mind going in different directions during race weeks.

EVERYONE IS DOWN at the truck this morning waiting on me. I'm a little surprised when I unlock the doors and Cammie jumps into the front seat, I figured Cody would be sitting up front today. I was also expecting twenty questions on the way to the track from my cousin, or at least glares from the back seat, but nothing. Cammie must not have told them anything, which it really isn't any of their business, but all the same I figured something would have been said.

I do notice my hand itching to reach across the center console and take her hand that is resting there, but instead I grip the steering wheel with both hands to keep from reaching out for her. Last night I may have convinced myself that this was all for the best, but this morning when I spotted her standing next to my truck, short denim shorts showing off those legs that I have had wrapped around me a couple times now, and a tank top that is showing off the shape of her breasts, reminding me of how nice they felt filling my hands, I'm definitely second-guessing the good idea part.

As the day goes on, she doesn't come out and watch the race. It annoys me that she watches Cody's but not mine. She works out my knee—I thought about just dealing with it, but my dad insisted. I couldn't keep from limping around after the second race so trying to convince my dad that I was all right wasn't going to work.

She asks questions in regards to my knee, keeping the conversation very professional. She looks me straight in the eyes when she speaks to me, but if you were anyone on the outside, you would never have guessed just two days before I was deep inside of her, those amazing legs wrapped tight around my waist, holding me inside of her. By the time she is finished with my knee, I'm absolutely sure I don't want things between us to be just professional, I want to be back inside of her. I want her to stand on the sidelines of the race watching, I want her to walk up to me and wrap her arms around my neck after a race and kiss me for all to see and envy me for because this beautiful woman is mine. A couple days, that's all I had and that's all it took, be damned with professional.

I'm about to tell her that when she moves away from me, wiping the oils she used to massage my knee off her hands with a towel. "All right, that should help a little for now. When we get back to the center in a couple days, I will start you on a daily schedule to work that knee, that should help with the next race. I didn't get much time before this race."

"Cam, we need to talk." I reach out for her arm, but she manages somehow in this very small room to avoid my hand.

She is out of the room before I can say anything else. She is avoiding me. If I know anything about Cammie, it's that she doesn't leave her work space without it being cleaned. She just dropped the towel she was using on the small counter that lines one small wall and walked right out. Hopping up off the table, I follow her out of the room. She must have gone outside, I want to follow her out and demand that she talk to me, but again I know that wouldn't work and I have realized all day that she is trying very hard not to bring our situation to the attention of everyone else. So instead I decide on a quick shower.

Showered and determined to find Cammie and talk to her, I walk out and find Cody surrounded by a group of women getting autographs. So much for talking with her now, because that same group seems to find their way over to me once they get from Cody what they wanted signed. Over their heads, I look up to find Cammie watching. I can't really tell what she is thinking, but last night I accused her of flirting with a guy who probably never even came within a couple of feet from her and here I am signing all kinds of body parts for these women. Krystal says something to her and she laughs, and something slams into my chest. She is trying to act like there is nothing wrong, but I can see it in her eyes as she watches me and there is no one to blame but myself, this is all me. She may have been the one to end it last night but I was the one to push her to do it.

My attention is pulled away when one of the kids that walked up starts asking questions. When I get a chance to look up again she is going into the bus with Krystal and my mom.

Cody makes his way over to me, still grabbing pictures that are being shoved in his direction to sign. "Are you going to tell me what's going on with you and Cammie?"

"What are you talking about?" I hand a signed poster back to a little girl.

"You guys aren't fooling anyone today, we all know something happened yesterday, it's driving Krystal insane. She has been trying to get Cammie to tell her all day, but she keeps dodging the subject."

I hand the last signed picture back to a young kid and watch as the group moves along to find the next rider. "So what, Krystal sends you to me hoping to get some information?"

"I'll be honest with you, I'm a little curious myself. One day you guys are all good, the next barely talking to one another. Come on, man, you didn't even join us for dinner last night. By the way, you missed a damn good steak."

"I screwed up," I admit out loud.

"What do you mean you screwed up, what did you do?"

"I accused her of being the reason I almost lost the first place spot in the race yesterday. It was wrong, I knew it was wrong even when the words were pouring out of my mouth last night, but I couldn't seem to stop them. I accused her of flirting with someone, that I'll be honest I knew she wasn't doing. She told me she wasn't going to be my excuse and called everything off. I can't blame her, I actually even tried to convince myself that she was right and that I needed to concentrate on this season, but then she showed up this morning in those damn shorts and I was a goner."

"Your dad got on your ass for almost allowing that rider to take you yesterday, didn't he?" Cody knows how my dad is, and even though he is right it's not a good excuse for the way I treated and blamed Cammie for it.

"He did, and I'm sure that fueled a little of my temper yesterday, but it was my fault. I came around the corner, saw the guy bent down to her and almost lost it there on the track. I lost my concentration."

"Wait," Cody's hands come up, stopping me, "Kade Maddox is a jealous boyfriend?"

"Trust me, not something I knew myself, but it cost me big time. She hasn't said too much to me today unless it's been professional."

"Give it some time and then what I've learned works best is groveling." Cody pats my back a couple times as he walks past me, heading in the direction of the bus.

"I don't want to become one of the groveling kind of guys," I say as he is walking away from me.

Cody stops, turning back to me laughing, "No man plans on becoming one of those groveling types, then that one woman comes into his life and even though it kills us the first couple of times, that wears off. Then you realize that in the morning you just wake up and the first thing out of your mouth is I'm sorry. You have no idea what for, but you know it will come in handy at some point in the day. That's the effect the right woman has on us, it's insane."

"Is it worth it?" I ask honestly.

"Absolutely." He turns and climbs the steps into the bus.

No hesitation, no stopping to think about it. I know what Cody has to deal with being in a relationship with Krystal and he answered that without a doubt in his mind. I love Krystal and I would do anything for her, she is family. She is kind-hearted and would give you the shirt off her back if you needed it, but she is always on the go, never sits still, and is strong-minded, very independent. All in all I know why Cody is in love with her. It's hard not to be.

Looking up at the bus, Cammie is sitting at the table, and our eyes lock. My arms twitch wanting to be around her, just holding her, those eyes that are always smiling aren't. They haven't all day. No matter how hard she is trying to convince everyone else that all is good, she isn't fooling me. Those eyes were the first thing I noticed about her. The blue in them change depending on her mood, they will tell a person everything they need to know if they just pay attention.

I have to try one last time. Hands in my pockets, I just stand there and stare up at her. With a nod of my head, I motion for her to come out and talk to me. She doesn't even think about it for a moment, she shakes her head no and turns away from me. I could just walk into the bus and confront her there in front of everyone, but I'm pretty sure that would do nothing but upset her more.

MY PLAN WAS to let Cammie have time, so I'm not sure how I end up in front of her hotel room, but here I stand waiting for her to answer the door. Cody mentioned groveling earlier, and I'm not going to lie, it may be a possibility if it gets her back in my arms. Just a couple nights with her and I've been spoiled. Trying to sleep last night without her next to me was near impossible, it felt empty and lonely. What this woman has done to me is something I swore would never happen to me. I thought all these men who fell to their knees for a woman had all lost their minds and their manhood, but I've joined the club. I'm not opposed to begging at this point.

I have to say I'm a little surprised when her hotel room door opens. I was expecting her to tell me to go away through the door, or just act like she wasn't there. "Can we talk?"

She doesn't open the door and invite me in. It's barely open and her head is resting against it, she looks exhausted. "Kade, there isn't really anything to talk about."

A young couple walks past us heading down the hallway, both staring as they pass by. "Cam, this isn't a conversation I think we need to have as an audience walks by, can I please come in? I promise to behave."

She is shaking her head no before I even finish asking the question. Fine, if she thinks I'm going to just walk away, she is wrong. We will have this conversation here in the hallway with an audience if that's what she wants, but we are going to talk.

"Cam, look, I'm sorry, let me just start there. I know what I said last night was wrong. I knew it even as I was saying it, but it still came out. I'm new to this relationship thing and never thought I'd be that type of guy who was jealous of men looking at someone I was with, but something slammed me in the chest yesterday when I rounded that corner and saw that guy bent down talking to you. I wanted to stop mid track and grab you and pull you away."

"Kade, that's all a little too caveman."

"Trust me, not a proud moment for me, I can tell you that. Then yes, my dad got on my ass for almost losing that race, I was mad and you were there, unfortunately you received the bad end of the deal. I'm sorry."

Bright blue eyes pierce into me for what feels like forever, I can see the war she is battling inside her own head, her eyes are like blue flames. Bracing myself with my hands on the doorframe, I lean into her, our faces only inches apart.

"Cam, it won't happen again." Leaning forward our lips brush, she doesn't move to close the remaining space between them, but she isn't pulling away from me either.

She closes her eyes, but they are closed tightly, that's what is holding me back from claiming her lips. Then it happens, she pulls away from me and my heart slams to the floor. She is shaking her head and what rocks me even harder are the tears I see in her eyes when she opens them.

"Kade, I'm sorry, but I can't. This season has so much riding on it for you and your family, for this race team. That's a lot to carry for one person and I've already seen what that is going to do to you. I'm not going to lie to you, I miss you already and I shouldn't miss you as much as I do, we haven't had that much time together, but that is what tells me the best thing for both of us is to keep this professional and nothing more. This season is only going to get harder for you, the pressure I already see your dad putting you through is going to be enough for you to have to handle, you don't need the relationship thing adding to that right now. Concentrate on being number one, you have worked so hard for this and I refuse to be any part that may cause that to not happen."

She surprises me when she closes the space between us once again, claiming my lips with hers. I can taste the salt from her tears on her lips and I can't keep myself from wrapping my arms around her waist and pulling her tightly into me. I deepen the kiss and have decided I'm not letting her go until she changes her mind.

That's when I hear the smallest whimper from her and her hands are at my chest pushing me away. Before I can say a word, or pull her back to me, I have the door closed in my face and my chest is ripped open. This is it, she is saying no. This feeling is like nothing I've ever felt before, everyone always hammered me about being the player and not settling down. Well, I've tried it, and it's not for me, this kind of emotion can't be healthy for anyone either.

THIS MORNING, the hardest thing to do was get out of bed and get ready for the next couple of days and the drive home. I'm pretty sure the confined space we are going to be traveling in for the next couple of days is going to be the hardest thing I'm ever going to have to do, being that close to Cammie and not being able to touch her.

Throwing my bag into the back of the truck, I turn to find Krystal and Cody walking over to the truck. "Where's Cammie? We need to get going," I ask as I take Krystal's suitcase and put it into the bed of the truck.

"Cammie is already gone." Krystal's answer is short and she turns to get into the truck.

"What do you mean gone?" I put my hand against the door to keep her from opening it.

"Gone, as in she isn't riding home with us."

I didn't get any sleep last night and I'm already irritated this morning, my cousin's little games aren't helping the matter right now.

"Krystal, where is Cammie?" My voice raises a little.

She arches an eyebrow at me. "All she said was that she had to get home quickly and was grabbing an early flight home. The text message was on my phone this morning when I woke up, that's all I know."

She decided to fly home instead of driving back with us. I would bet my bike that she didn't have to rush home. I'm convinced now that Cody and every other man who puts themselves into a relationship with one woman is completely insane.

CHAPTER SEVENTEEN

CAMMIE

Three weeks! Three weeks of hell is maybe what I should say. After I shut the door on Kade that last night in Las Vegas I knew there was no way I was going to be able to handle driving all the way back to Texas with him. I could have asked Tracey and Michael if I could just ride back in the bus with them, but I couldn't come up with a good enough excuse as to why I wouldn't want to ride back with Kade, Krystal and Cody without telling them the truth. My next option was to fly home. I found a flight that was leaving at four that morning and called Lucas to ask if he could pick me up at the airport once in Texas. Of course that led to me having to tell him what happened between Kade and I, but he is my best friend, those are the things you don't keep from a best friend. I didn't give him the whole story, though. Kade and Lucas are friends, and I don't want him to think he needs to pick between a friendship with either of us.

My phones vibrates in my pocket. Pulling it out, Lucas's face is showing with a new text message.

Lucas: I'm here at the track watching the guys.

The past three weeks I have been avoiding any area that Kade is in unless absolutely a need was presented for us to be around each other, that is other than when he comes in to get worked on. So, other than a meeting that Michael requires us all to be at, there isn't much need for us to be around each other. Nothing has been harder than to act like everything is good when we are around everyone.

Every time we are in the same room together it gets harder and harder to remember why I decided a relationship of any kind other than professional was a bad idea, but then I walk outside to meet up with my best friend and see the reason why I'm able to keep control of myself when we are alone together, Brooke!

Since we have been back, Kade doesn't seem bothered at all. In fact, Brooke has been hanging out more and more, which is driving everyone else around the center completely crazy, not just me. Kade, on the other hand, takes every moment he can to show her all the attention she is begging for.

We leave in four days for another race, this time to my relief Lucas is joining us. I was extremely excited when he told me he was coming. I get along great with Krystal and Cody, but I still feel a little like the outsider sometimes. Then Lucas told me his girlfriend would be coming along as well. Jenna is great, they have been together now for almost a year, but it means I'm the spare wheel again.

Lucas is standing next to Michael in full conversation, but both have their eyes on Kade as he comes around the corner and flies past them for another lap. I watch as Michael points something out to Lucas, I can't hear anything that is being said but Lucas nods his head in agreement.

I stand back and watch. Cody comes around and I notice him flexing his arm and favoring his elbow as he makes his way through the whoops. I make a mental note to ask him about that later. He hasn't mentioned any problems with his elbow, but it's something I don't want getting worse before he decides it is a problem and it's harder to fix.

I need to be out here more, watching the guys while they are training. For one, I get a better idea of the strains they put on different parts of their bodies, for two, if I don't see it for myself and because they are both very stubborn, something might go too far and then take them out for the season. My job is to make sure that doesn't happen to either of them. Being out here more and watching them will tell me everything they aren't telling me.

"Cammie, how long have you been standing there?" Lucas walks over to me and wraps me in a big bear hug.

"Not long, I'm just watching the guys as they ride by, actually doing my job."

"Cammie, today I'm noticing Cody favoring his left arm a little." Michael walks over to me as well.

Nodding, I agree with Michael. "I just noticed that myself. I've already made a mental note of that. Have him come into the training room and I'll chat with him about it. I'll make sure to be out here more during training to watch. Seems that if they aren't going to tell me when something is wrong, I'm going to have to pay a little closer attention."

Michael pats Lucas on the shoulder. "Lucas, I can't thank you enough for suggesting Cammie to us, she is on top of everything."

Michael turns away from us and heads back over to the track. He waits for Cody to come around again and signals for him to come in. I watch as Cody nods to what Michael is saying then takes off onto the track once again.

"So, are you ready for Florida?" Lucas asks, standing next to me.

"There are a few things that need to be done, but mostly I'm ready, yes. I'm just glad you are coming along for this one. Don't get me wrong, everyone here is great and Krystal and I have become great friends, but still feel a little like an outsider sometimes."

Lucas wraps an arm around my shoulders. "Trust me, it won't take much longer for you to feel like part of the family, plus I'm with you guys for the remaining races of the season, my schedule just got cleared the other day at work."

Hearing the sound of tires braking and sliding across the dirt have both of us turning our attention back to the track. The dust is thick, but through it I see Kade as he takes off his helmet. Our eyes lock for a minute and if I didn't know any better I'd swear he just glared at Lucas, but just as quickly Brooke is by his side wrapped around him.

Michael's shoulders puff up a little and he shakes his head, I'm sure out of irritation, but he turns his attention back to the track and Cody, who is still taking laps.

"No one likes that woman, I don't even think Kade likes her."

Lucas speaks next to me, bringing my attention back to Kade just in time to see Brooke wrap herself around him and claim his lips. My breath catches in my chest. It feels like someone just punched me right in the center of my breasts. Kade's eyes lock with mine, I can't stand here and watch this anymore.

"I have some stuff to put up in the training room, if you want to stay out here that's fine."

Lucas doesn't answer me. When I finally tear my eyes away from Kade's and look over at Lucas, I'm surprised to see anger etched across his face and it's directed right at Kade.

"Hey, look at me." I step in front of him and into his line of sight.

His eyes quickly soften when they meet mine. "I'll come in and help you out." He wraps his arm once again over my shoulder and we turn together, away from the disgusting sight of PDA happening in front of us.

. . .

FOLDING the final towel I just pulled out of the dryer and putting them away in the cabinet, I grab a sheet and throw it over at Lucas.

"Can you put that over the exam table, please? Cody should be coming in soon. Then after I finish with him I need to run out to the trailer and make sure everything is stocked and ready before they leave in the morning."

The race next weekend is in Florida. The truck and trailer along with the bus will be leaving tomorrow to drive there, we will all be flying out on Tuesday.

Lucas takes the sheet and lays it over the table. He hasn't said much since we got back. "Are you all right?" I finally ask him.

"I can kick his ass for you, all you need to do is ask. Actually, you don't have to even ask, I'm good with just doing it."

Lucas and I haven't talked much about Kade and me. I told him a little the day he picked me up from the airport, but since then not much. One thing I have always loved about Lucas is that he doesn't push for information either, when I need to talk he is there, but other than that he never pushes a subject.

"Why would I ask you to kick his ass?" I try to give my best smile like I have no idea what he could be talking about.

Walking over to me, he places his hands on each of my shoulders. "Cammie, I know you told me that whatever was between you two was small and brief, but I saw the look in your eyes today, you aren't telling me everything."

"There wasn't much to tell, plus you and Lucas are friends. I'm not going to get between that and have you pick sides. Yes, we tried something, not even sure what you would have called it, but it didn't work out, nothing more to tell really."

"First off, you never have to wonder which side I would take when it comes between you and Kade. Yes, Kade and I are friends, but you and I are much closer. Being Kade's friend, I also know that when he was staring you down like he was out there he was throwing it up in your face and that I'm not all right with at all. I have no problem punching the guy."

Lucas, my protector. Has been since we met. Even though I tried to tell him many, many times I'm more than capable of handling my own battles, he has always been there taking the role of a big brother. Wrapping my arms around his waist, I hug him tight.

"I'm good, Lucas, I promise," I speak against his chest. It's much easier to lie to him if I don't have to look him straight in the eyes.

The doors to the training center fly open and slam hard against the inside walls. Jumping, I look around Lucas to see Kade standing in the doorway.

"Am I interrupting something?" He isn't even looking at me, he is glaring at Lucas.

Lucas's arms tighten around me, not in a possessive way but in protection. By the way Kade's jaw is flexing he isn't seeing it in a protective way.

My hands itch to touch that jaw as I watch the muscle flex a couple of times. I need to get a grip, I just watched this guy make out with another woman as he stared me down with a challenging look. Then to top it off he thinks he can just barge into the room.

Pulling myself out of Lucas's arms, I stand to my full height, my shoulders back. "Do you need something, Kade?"

Kade's eyes stay directed over my head and at Lucas. "Kade!" I yell at him this time.

It takes him a couple more seconds but he finally looks down at me. "My knee needs to be worked out."

"All right, but you are going to have to wait. Cody will be coming in shortly and I have to run out to the trailer after that to make sure everything is stocked before it gets too late. I can let you know when I get back in here and you can come in then."

"Lucas, can you give us a minute? I need to talk to Cammie." His eyes never leave mine as he speaks to Lucas.

I feel Lucas take a protective step closer behind me. Kade and I need to clear a few things up, it's time all of this stopped.

Turning around, I look up at my best friend. "Hey, give us a minute, all right? It's all good, I'm a big girl and no matter what you believe, I can take care of myself." I tease with him, hoping to take some of the tension out of the air.

Lucas gives me a small smile. "He hasn't figured out what a little hell cat you are yet, has he?" He leans down and gives me a small kiss on the forehead. "I'll be right outside."

Kade waits for the door to close behind Lucas. "What's all of that about?" Kade motions with his head toward the door that Lucas just left through. "I knew there was something more than just friendship between the two of you."

Really, we are going down that road again? Now he is accusing me of being more than friends with Lucas. I'm not feeding into it this time.

"What do you want, Kade?"

"I want to know what's going on between you and Lucas." His voice is starting to raise.

"What right do you have to even ask that question? What difference does it make to you?"

Kade closes the space between us. Putting my hands up, I stop him when they hit his chest. "Stop, Kade. You have no right to ask anything about my personal life. Besides that, you know Lucas has a girlfriend who he loves a great deal. There are no words to express how much Lucas means to me, feelings like that would be lost on you."

"Best friends? Really? When I walked in, you looked pretty comfy in his arms. Does Jenna know how close you two are?"

"Are you kidding me right now? You just had your tongue

shoved down the throat of a woman you are just using. You have no right to worry about me or Lucas, or any arms that I may be in."

I try to take a step back from him, but his arms circles around my waist and I'm pulled tight against his chest. His jaw flexes, damn that jaw! My hand comes up before I even realize what I'm doing and my fingers run along his jaw line.

"Cam, I need you," he whispers against my lips before he claims them.

My body instantly melts into his and my fingers dig a little more into the side of his face. Then it hits me. Something fruity, and the smell of something floral. I want to gag, but more I'm pissed at myself for allowing this to happen.

Pushing myself away, my hand goes from clutching onto his jaw to slapping him across the same cheek.

"Get out of here, now." I'm fighting the tears. I'm hurt, but more than that I'm pissed, with myself.

"Cammie, please." He takes a step toward me again.

Taking a couple steps back and completely out of his reach, I wrap my arms around my stomach, I feel sick. "Go back to Brooke and leave me alone."

I wait a few seconds, but realize he isn't moving. Fine, if he isn't leaving then I am. Walking wide around him and staying out of touching distance, I quickly leave the room. No one is in the hallway, not even Lucas, but I'm relieved. Even though Lucas told me he would be right outside, I'm glad he isn't. I need to get away from everyone right now, especially Kade. I obviously can't trust myself around him. I just allowed him to kiss me and he tasted and smelled of Brooke. What makes me even more pissed off is that if I stayed I can't say I wouldn't have walked back into his arms again.

CHAPTER EIGHTEEN

KADE

I should go after her, but I can't get my feet to move. Looking around the room, anger at myself flares. Grabbing the side of the table, I flip it over and end up kicking it across the room until it hits the wall.

The door behind me flies open and Lucas comes barging in looking ready to pounce. He frantically looks around the room. "Where the hell is Cammie?"

Did he honestly think I would hurt Cammie? Now I'm pissed at Lucas. I know he is upset with me right now, but I would hope he would know I'd never lay a hand on a woman.

"Damn it, Kade, where is Cammie?" he asks once again.

"Calm down, she left. Do you honestly think I would have hurt her?"

Lucas takes a couple deep breaths and looks around the room, his eyes land on the table I kicked across the room. "All right, if Cammie isn't going to tell me everything that happened between the two of you, maybe you should. This isn't like either of you. Sure, you are a player, but that shit you pulled out at the track while you had Brooke's tongue down your throat was low. I may not agree with your playboy attitude with women, but you aren't usually that big of an ass hat, so start explaining."

I'm about to tell Lucas to mind his own business, but after taking a couple deep breaths and calming down a little I realize he is completely right. Walking over, I pick the table up that I kicked across the room, thankful I didn't break it, having to explain that to my dad or Cammie wouldn't have been good. Placing it back in its spot, I sit down on it.

"She is driving me crazy," I finally admit out loud.

"Care to explain a little better than that?" Lucas props himself up against the cabinet across from me, folding his arms across his chest.

"Look, I know you two are best friends and all, but I'm not sure how much you tell each other, so I'm going to give you the short, PG version. From the moment I met Cammie something has drawn me to her. I tried to fight it, but the day that box fell onto her was the day I realized fighting the pull toward her wasn't working. I mean, damn, I know you two are best friends, I know you are in love with Jenna, but when you get too close, or when I walk in and see you holding her, I want to tear you apart if I'm being honest. Anyway, we decided fighting the pull between us wasn't working so we stopped fighting it and all I'm going to say is it was good..."

Lucas puts his hand up to stop me. "If you don't want my fist in your face, probably better you stop there with the good part."

"Sorry, anyway. Short version, first race, I thought someone was flirting with her, then I almost lost the first place because I was concentrating on her and then my dad got on my ass, and well, I blamed her that night. She called it off between us, I agreed at first, but then realized I didn't want to call it off, tried once more, she turned me down and here we are."

Lucas just stands there nodding his head. "So you thought it would be a good idea to have Brooke around to what, make

Cammie jealous? Glaring her down as you made out with another woman seemed like a good way to get her back?"

"You said it, ass hat," I say, pointing at myself.

"Then you come barging in here, accusing us of being in a relationship. Man, you are batting a thousand right now. Do I want to know why she isn't here right now? What happened after I left?"

Hanging my head down, I know if I tell him about all of it, he probably will punch me. "We kissed."

Silence fills the room. When I look up Lucas is standing there waiting on me to continue. "Let's just say the jealous side came out again and I said things I shouldn't, things that yes, you should probably punch me for."

He points a hand toward me. "From the look of that much redder side of your face, I'm going to guess Cammie already took a swing at you."

Getting up from the table, I walk over to a mirror that is hanging on the wall and examine the side of my face that Cammie slapped. "It stings a little, she has quite a swing on her."

"She has a little bit of fire in her," Lucas agrees with me.

"You should have taken a couple of swings at me."

Again, he nods in agreement. "Probably should, but that may make you feel better about it and I'm not wanting you to feel better just yet."

"I should probably go and find her, apologize."

Lucas shakes his head no. "You are the last person she needs to be around right now. You need to work on fixing things, first off getting rid of Brooke. She is driving everyone crazy around here, stop trying to make Cammie jealous. Look, Kade, we are friends. I know you and I know this isn't like you, it's the only reason I'm not running after Cammie and telling her to stay far away from you. I know what a woman can do to a man, and the things he will do that just aren't his norm, but I can also promise you this. One more situation like today, I will not hold back from beating the shit out of you. That is a promise, not a threat. Cammie means the world to me and I will pick her over you anytime of the day."

"Just to make sure I'm clear on what you are saying. You are all right if I try to patch things up with Cammie?"

Lucas's laughs and pushes himself away from the counter. "Cammie is a big girl and can make decisions for herself. If you for one second think this is going to be easy, you are so very wrong. She is going to pull you through the ringer and back, and that alone is what makes me all right with this."

Lucas heads for the door. "Hey, man, again, I'm sorry," I apologize once again.

He holds the door so that it doesn't close behind him. "I'm going to go find Cammie, if there is anyone you need to apologize to it's her, and just saying sorry probably isn't going to cut it. Make it count this time."

Before I can respond the door shuts, leaving me in the room alone. Apologize to Cammie, without just using the words, I think I'm going to be finding out what Cody was talking about when he mentioned groveling. I'm pretty sure I'm going to have to go to Cammie on my knees to beg her to forgive me this time.

The door opens again, but it isn't Cammie, it's Cody. "Hey, man, is Cammie here? Your dad sent me in."

"She had to run out to the trailer and check on supplies before they leave in the morning, she should be back shortly."

"All right, well I'll just wait in my room then, if you can tell her to come get me. By the way, Brooke is sitting out there pouting and your dad won't let her back here. You might want to go out there."

"Sure, thanks." Dealing with Brooke is the last thing I want to do, but it's my fault she is here and I need to go and handle it. First step in making things right with Cammie, even if she has no idea.

Walking down the hallway, I can hear Brooke and my dad outside the door. "You know no one is allowed except members of this team. So you can either wait outside in the car or leave altogether," I hear my dad say as I walk through the double doors.

"Finally, tell your father to let me back there." Brooke points at the doors I just came through.

"If Dad says no one but team members then that's the way it goes." I look over at my dad. "Sorry, Dad, I got this from here."

Dad just nods and walks through the doors, I'm going to have to apologize to him as well. Damn, I screwed things up good.

Brooke takes a step closer and tries to wrap her arms around my waist. I take a step back, holding out my hand to stop her where she is. "There is no way for me to say any of this that isn't going to make me sound like a huge jerk, so I'm just going to say it. Brooke, you can no longer hang out over here at the center. We have had our fun times, but it's got to stop now."

"What are you saying, Kade?" Her voice is doing that whining, high-pitched sound and it's grinding on my nerves.

"I'm saying whatever we had going on between us is over."

Brooke puts her hands on her hips and glares over at me. "This is about that woman who works here, isn't it?"

"It's about me telling you that it just isn't working, I'm sorry."

"You are sorry, really, Kade. You always come back, but this next time maybe I won't be so willing to take you back."

I have nothing else to say, so I just give her a nod, let her take it as she wants. That's when I really look at her for the first time since coming back out and once again I'm the cause of the pain I see in a female's eyes. Sure, Brooke can be a little hard to get along with, but I think she is really hurt by me basically throwing her out of the training center and telling her to never come back. I've been selfish and that needs to stop. Someone needs to beat the crap out of me.

Brooke turns and stomps her way out of the center altogether. Through the door that leads from the inside track to outside, I can see when her car peels out of the parking lot.

Walking back through the doors, I find my dad leaning up against the wall waiting for me, I assume.

"So you heard?"

"Son, that woman's voice is hard not to hear. I'm not going to lie, everyone will be relieved to hear she won't be hanging out anymore, but son..."

"I know, Dad, I've been an ass hat. At least that is what Lucas called me today."

"Son, no one around here has been blind to what is going on between Cammie and you. No one knows the full story, but we all know it isn't good. Cammie is trying, but after that stunt you pulled earlier I wanted to pull you away and beat the crap out of you. Your mother and I didn't raise you to treat any person the way you have been treating people the last few weeks. Sure, you were spoiled, more of that came from your grandmother, and you are definitely hot-headed, but you have never disrespected anyone like you have people lately."

"Dad, I'm sorry. I know that's an easy word to throw around but I do mean it. Things are going to change, I'm sorry that I've disappointed you guys, I'm finding my way back and I promise things are changing."

"Son, women do strange things to us men, trust me when I say we have all been in the 'ass hat' category more than once."

THE WEEKEND SEEMS to creep by. I have to stop myself more than a few times from calling Cammie and asking her to meet with me so we can talk. Lucas thinks it's best if I give her a little time and he knows her better than anyone else so I take his advice. It doesn't stop me from ordering her some flowers to be delivered on Monday to the center, though. I know it's cheesy and she might either deny them or throw them at me but I figure it's a start to a very long apology.

CHAPTER NINETEEN

CAMMIE

It's Monday and I have been hiding out in my office all morning. Over the weekend Lucas called me a couple of times asking how I was doing and trying to get me to go out with him and Jenna and some friends but I was pretty sure I wouldn't be any fun to be around.

"Cammie, these were just delivered for you. Michael said the delivery man just dropped them off, asked if I would bring them in." Tracy walks into my office carrying a ridiculously large bouquet of white roses all tipped in a different color and a bear wearing riding gear wrapped around the vase.

She sets them down on my desk and looks at them with pride. These can only be from one person and she seems to know who that person his, her son. So I have to hold back my need to roll my eyes and chuck the flowers into the trash.

"Thank you, Tracy, for bringing them in to me."

I know she wants to say something but she doesn't, she just turns and leaves.

I have to admit, he has great taste, the flowers are beautiful. It's one of the reasons I haven't dropped them into the trash can yet.

The second is just my curiosity. There's a card and I want to know what he has to say, it's probably something simple, but I need to know.

Pulling the envelope from the flowers, I slowly pull the card out.

Cam,

There is one rose for each of the times I know that I'm going to have to come groveling on my knees asking for forgiveness before I will be able to be forgiven. I've been wrong these past few weeks and I plan to make it up to you. I am not giving up, I need you to be mine!

Your Rider,

Kade

FLIPPING THE CARD OVER, I find there is more.

A shift in life is never expected, but can hold amazing possibilities!

I have no words to express how I'm feeling right now. Sitting down in my chair, I read both sides of the card over and over. This is a side of Kade I wasn't prepared for, a groveling side.

His words, I need you to be mine, run over and over in my head. Lucas told me that he and Kade had a talk after I ran out the other day. He wouldn't tell me everything that was said, but he did tell me that Kade hadn't been himself the past few weeks. He was defending him which, to be honest, surprised me a little. It piqued my curiosity as well and I wanted to ask what exactly was said between them but decided if he wanted to tell me he would have.

I jump when Krystal surprises me, her head popping through the door of my office. "Holy cow, what did he do wrong this time? That's one heck of an apology." She comes over and sniffs the flowers.

"How do you know who they are from?"

"Cammie, you and Kade may think no one notices what's going on between the two of you but we all see it. You two are crazy about each other and everyone else seems to know except the two of you. I wouldn't believe for a minute that you were seeing anyone else right now, I see the look in your eyes when you think no one is watching. I'm curious what he did, though."

I play with the card in my hand. I have Lucas who is a great best friend, but it's hard sometimes to have certain conversations with him. Krystal and I have become pretty close and it would be nice to have another woman to talk to. Sam is going through some major life changes of her own right now and I haven't mentioned anything about what has been going on here to her.

Stretching out my hand toward Krystal, I hold the card out to her. "This came with the flowers."

Krystal takes the card, I watch as her eyes widen as she reads the words. Her eyes are huge with disbelief when she looks up at me.

I signal with my hand, "Turn it over."

"You mean there is more?" She flips the card over and covers her mouth with her hand in surprise.

"All right, maybe these aren't from my cousin, there is no way he came up with these words." She hands the card back to me. "What the heck happened?"

I'm not ready to get into all of the details with her on what happened in here on Friday, no matter how close I think we may be, he is still her family. "Let's just say he made quite the ass out of himself."

"So did you hear that he told Brooke not to come back to the center?"

"Yes, Cody told me the other day when he came in. I guess he was in his room, the door was open and he overheard a little of what was said."

"I can't say anyone will miss that woman, but if I have to be honest I do feel a little sorry for her."

I have nothing to say, so I just stare at the flowers.

"Are you going to forgive him?"

Shrugging my shoulders, I just rock back and forth in my chair. That is something I can't answer right now.

"Well, I came in for a reason. Food! Uncle Michael ordered pizza and it just arrived, let's go eat."

Krystal turns and heads out of my office before I can say a word. I can't hide in here all day. Opening the top drawer of my desk, I slip the card from the flowers inside and get up to follow Krystal.

Walking into the meeting/lunch room, everyone else is already there and eating, even Kade. Our eyes meet the moment I walk through the door. His are uncertain and that softens me a little more. He isn't sure how I'm going to react to the flowers.

"It's about time you two got in here. If you would have been any longer there may not have been any left." Cody gives Krystal a kiss on the cheek when she sits down next to him.

"Well, someone gave Cammie an amazing bouquet of flowers," Krystal announces and my cheeks instantly heat up.

Looking around the table, there is only one seat left and that is next to Kade. I'm pretty sure it was planned that way, maybe not by Kade, but by everyone else. Everyone seems to be on Team Kade.

"So the groveling has finally begun." Cody shoves another bite of his pizza in his mouth, smiling over at Kade, until Krystal smacks him the stomach.

"Why did you hit me? I only said what everyone else is thinking." Cody points around the table.

I can't help but laugh a little.

"All right, stop giving Kade and Cammie a hard time, we have flight information to discuss for tomorrow and I need all of you to pay attention." Michael ends the teasing and brings a little order back to the room.

Kade leans over, "I meant every word on that card." His hot breath tickles my ear and the heat shoots through my body to my core.

I'm going to have to get a little self-restraint around this man, I cannot make it this easy for him. When I turn my face to look at him, our lips are only inches apart. "Thank you for the flowers, they are beautiful."

His eyes bounce from my lips to my eyes and then back to my lips. Quickly I turn my attention back to the pizza on my plate, before I forget there are other people in the room.

DURING LUNCH I try to keep my attention anywhere other than on Kade. He doesn't push for conversation either. It's a relief and frustrating at the same time. This is going to be hard. A part of me hates him for how he threw Brooke in my face, but it's a small part and getting smaller and smaller by the moment. Any time I look at the flowers I think about the words he wrote on the card, my chest tightens every time I think of the words on the back.

A shift in life is never expected! Since the day I walked onto the grounds of this training center my life shifted. Starting with who I was working for. Something about Kade, since the moment I met him, has drawn me to him. Even through all of that playboy exterior, I've had a pull toward him. I fought it, only to give in, then heart break after only a couple days. Everything that has happened in the last month should be enough to keep me away, but no, here I am sitting with the butterflies in my stomach over him telling me on his card that I will be his.

Do I want to be his? If I'm being completely honest with myself, yes! I'm tired of fighting this draw to him, but then he goes and does things like blaming me for having a bad race, or shoves other women in front of me to make me jealous.

Looking up at the clock, it's already two. The boys were going to run for a couple of hours then come in for a rub down and call it a day early. We all have to be at the airport at four in the morning for our flight to Florida. Kade is going to come in and soak in an ice bath, while I work out Cody's arm that he has been favoring. Cody being in here will help put a barrier between Kade and any temptation I may want to give into.

I take a deep breath of relief when Cody walks in first. "Hey, Cammie, Kade said he will be in shortly, he had to go and talk to Michael about something and wanted to grab a quick shower."

"That's fine, the ice bath is all ready for him when he gets here, let's start on that arm. How is it feeling today after riding?"

Cody sits down on the table and starts bending his arm. "Actually better today, it's still a little tender, but definitely feeling better since you worked it out last time and today I wore the brace you gave me to wear."

"Good, sounds like we caught it before it caused a permanent injury. I hate to say it but you will always have issues with your elbows and knees after doing this kind of profession. The shock those parts of your body absorbs during a race is intense."

Cody shrugs his shoulders, "It will be lots of fun in the meantime."

"What's going to be a lot of fun?" Kade walks in and goes straight over to the ice bath.

"Cammie is explaining how old my body is going to feel once my racing career is over," Cody throws over his shoulder toward Kade.

I can't help but watch over Cody's head as Kade pulls his shirt up and over his head. The way his back muscles flex as he turns and drops the shirt in a nearby chair. My breath hitches as my eyes travel down to the "V" at the lower section of his back and disappears under the waistband of his shorts. My hands tingle and I want to run my hands from the top of his shoulder blades, down to that "V" section on his lower back.

Cody's laugh brings my attention back to the work I'm supposed to be concentrating on at this moment. My face instantly goes red as I bring my eyes down to the work I'm doing on his arm, I can't look him in the eye right now.

"Shut up, Cody."

"You need to give up on denying him if the pressure you just had as you massaged my arm is any indication as to what might be going through your mind right now."

"Cody..." I try to keep my voice down.

If I wasn't holding onto his arm, I'm pretty sure he would have fallen off the table from laughing so hard. It's almost worth releasing his arm and having him fall to the floor, but right now Kade doesn't seem to be paying attention to what is going on between Cody and me. His head is relaxed back against the side of the tub and his eyes are closed. I'm surprised, because Cody's laugh is filling the room and I know if he looked over he would wonder what was going on because by the heat I'm feeling through my body, I can only guess how red my face is.

"Relax, Cammie, he has his ear buds in, he isn't hearing a thing I'm saying," he wipes the tears away from his eyes. "How long are you going to make him grovel?"

"Why does everyone think I need to forgive him so easily? A few days ago he had Brooke all draped around him. He blames me for having a bad race, he is temperamental. Then, one day he decides he may be acting like a spoiled teenager and sends me flowers and everyone thinks I need to just forget everything and jump back into his arms."

Letting go of his arm, I let it drop back to his side, then turn away and walk over to the cabinet with all the oils lined inside. Pushing all the bottles around, looking for nothing in particular,

I'm trying to decide if I'm upset at everyone else, or myself. It's driving me insane that I want to so easily go back to him. That every time we are in the same room I feel the pull between us. Even now, it's hard not to forget Cody is in the room as well and just walk over and run my hands over his back and those muscles that I probably already have completely memorized.

"Cody, can you give us a minute?" I jump at the sound of Kade's voice right behind me.

Damn it, he heard everything. Probably heard everything Cody said as well. Cody doesn't answer, but I hear the sound of the door opening, and then closing.

My hands are braced on the counter, my head hanging down. I can't turn around, there is nothing but temptation standing behind me, wet temptation at that, and I'm more embarrassed now than I was when Cody called me out.

"Cammie, we need to talk."

A chill runs over my body. He is close, very close. I can now feel the heat from his body mixed with a chill from the ice cold water he was sitting in.

"Please back up some, Kade."

Damn it, I hear the begging in my voice. You know what? Screw this, I can't keep all of this up. He wants to talk, I'm going to talk.

Straightening, I turn on him so quickly that he takes a couple steps back which ends up giving me a little more breathing room and a lot more confidence.

"Fine, you want to talk, well me first. I'm not going to stand here and tell you I have no feelings toward you, or that every time we are in the room together I can easily forget if there is anyone else in the room and all I want to do is wrap myself around you. There is a pull between us and I feel it every time we are within probably a hundred feet from each other. You can be standing outside the door and I sense you there, every nerve in my body comes alive, my heart kicks up a couple notches, I want to be naked and pressed against you so bad that every time I think of you my core heats up, my knees get weak and I think about jumping into that ice bath just to calm down. But even with all that said, I'm still thinking it's a better idea that we keep things professional. You have way too much riding on this season and to be honest, I love this job and don't want to get fired!"

CHAPTER TWENTY

KADE

That blazing blue color is dancing in her eyes right now. They remind me of when fire is so hot it's blue and it's when her eyes blaze with that color I find that I have the hardest time not reaching out and showing her in great detail everything I want to do to her body. Now isn't the time for that.

"Are you finished?"

Her chest is expanding rapidly, like it does after we have amazing sex. I really need to get my head out of that department of thinking. I need her to trust me again. I'm pretty sure I'm not going to be able to convince her I want more than just a physical relationship with her if I attack her every time I see her.

"I will talk with everyone and tell them to stop making comments about you forgiving me if you would like me to."

"Damn it, Kade, no." She leans back against the counter looking defeated, the fight draining from her face. "I don't want you saying anything to anyone, kind of what I'm trying to get at is I wish it didn't have to be everyone's business."

"Cammie, this is a family business. At least five days of the week we are all here at this center, we have no lives, so the only choice we have is to get involved with each other's. No one is meaning to pressure you, I assure you. Look at it this way, at least you know they like you."

"I guess I should be looking at it that way." She gives me a small smile.

I can't hold back from her any longer. Taking a couple steps to close the space between us, I grab her around the shoulders and pull her tight into my chest and just hold her. It takes a moment, but her arms wrap around my waist and she lays her head against my chest.

"I'm sorry if the flowers caused too much attention today, I swear the only thought on my mind when I ordered them was an apology." My chin rests on top of her head as I talk. Surprisingly I'm content to just hold her right now.

"They are beautiful, thank you. I especially like the bear in the riding gear, with your jersey number on it. They have those just sitting around the flower shop?" She pulls herself out of my arms and leans against the counter again.

No matter how badly I want to pull her back to me, I decide giving her a little space would be the better idea, so I take a step back.

"No, actually, those were a promotional thing a couple years back, we have a few floating around here so I asked my mom to add it before she brought them in here."

She hasn't mentioned the card. "Cam, I meant every word written on that card, though."

Her eyes go wide and a small tint of red touches her cheeks, she looks down at the floor.

"I know you believe we need to keep things professional. You are right, I do have a lot riding on this season and my family is depending on me. Back in Vegas, I was feeling that pressure. There is no excuse for blaming you and I knew that from the moment the words came out of my mouth but I couldn't take them back. Then we have had the last three weeks home and my biggest mistake is when I decided to use Brooke. It was wrong of me in so many different ways. Honestly, my first reason was not to make you jealous, I was hoping it would help me forget about being with you, but I should have known better. The other day when we kissed, I realized something very important. I like the way I feel when I have you in my arms. I like the feel of your hand in mine, your lips against mine, your body naked against mine. I need you to be mine. You want to keep it professional and I'm telling you I'm going to do whatever I need to do and no matter how long it takes, you will be mine, Cam."

My knees about buckle as I watch her eyes go to a crystal white blue. The color of pleasure, want, desire and need. "Don't look at me like that, Cam, I'm trying very hard right now to not grab you and take you on that table," I point to the massage table behind me, "or against that counter," I look at the counter behind her.

I have to hide a smile when I see her raging a war within herself. She wants me just as bad as I want her. She takes in a very deep breath and closes her eyes, I watch and I notice her knuckles turning white from holding onto the counter tightly.

After a few seconds she finally releases the breath she was holding and her arms fall to her sides. When she opens her eyes, they have some deeper blue colors threaded through them now.

"Kade, I can't be the excuse if you don't have a winning season."

Nodding, I agree with her as she speaks. "I know this. I also know that the only thing that is going to convince you of this is to show you and that's exactly what I'm planning on doing, Cammie. I understand this season is important to my family, trust me, there isn't a day my father lets me forget it."

"Exactly, I'm not saying that I don't believe you are serious about this thing you want between us, but I've also witnessed the intensity between your father and you. I will not become the fall guy again, Kade. You won't mean for it to happen but it will."

"I have a different outlook on this season now, Cammie. There are two races I'm going to win. One on that bike and one with your heart."

Something changes in her. I can't really explain it, but her shoulders seem to lighten a little, her back straightens and there is a small smile on her lips. She looks a little more relaxed, I would say almost a little playful. "Then prove it."

A challenge, that's all the invite I need. Closing the space between us once again, I look straight down at her. I'm not going to touch her, one of the hardest things I've ever had to do, but I'm going to do exactly what she is asking me to do, prove it.

Her eyes move from my lips to my eyes and then back to my lips again. This may be one of the hardest things I've ever had to do, but the reward will be so worth it.

"Just remember, I don't lose." Our lips are so close that while I speak, mine brush hers.

"I'm counting on it."

I need to walk away before I'm unable to control myself. I need to go and jump back into that ice bath, but instead I kiss her on the forehead and start to back away from her. That white-blue color is back and I'm about to give in, but if I'm going to get her to understand my feelings for her then I'm going to have to prove there is more than just the physical attraction between us.

My knee isn't going to get massaged tonight, her hand on any part of my body is too much of a temptation right now. Turning, I make my way to the door. "I'll see you in the morning, Cam."

I try to casually walk out of the room, but the door seems miles away and if I don't put some distance between the two of us fast I may not be leaving this room until I've bent her over that massage table and fulfilled my need to be deep inside her again.

"Kade," she calls to me just as I push the door open. Turning around, I see her for the first time in weeks smiling, like a real smile and relaxed. That's a good start.

"I wouldn't have been able to say no to you."

My hand tightens on the handle of the door to keep me from stalking back over to her. "This isn't me saying no to you. It's me showing you I'm racing for your heart."

Turning, I leave the room, letting the door shut behind me. I would have gone straight to my truck and left, putting distance between us but I'm in only my boxer briefs and a towel from sitting in the ice bath. I left my shorts and shirt laying in the room and going back in there for them isn't an option right now, so I make my way back to my room. It will be soon, I have to keep telling myself that.

IT'S two-thirty in the morning, and normally I probably would have grumbled to my parents about booking us such an early flight, but this morning I am up and waiting for the van impatiently.

Lucas, Cody, even my dad has warned me more times than I can remember that when that one woman comes into your life, you are willing to make changes you never dreamt you would consider. I would laugh at them, find me a girl for the evening and pity them for wanting to spend all of their time with one girl. I had my life tracked out, this season I was going to be number one and no one, especially a woman, was going to knock me off that track. Damn, was I wrong!

Not that I'm off track, it's only been one race and I did finish first, but I learned something else that weekend. A woman is going to change my life. No, what I mean is a woman has changed my life! The last three weeks when Brooke was around I was trying to convince myself I'm good with my old way of life. A woman for a little companionship at night, maybe a fun night out, but that was really all. Then, the other day when I was kissing Brooke in front of Cammie, I found out I was determined to prove to myself, more that to Cammie that I was good with our relationship being professional, but when I looked over and saw the pain in Cammie's eyes, no words could explain the pain in my chest. Brooke felt wrong on so many levels and I knew from that moment I was no longer all right with my old life.

It's official, I'm one of those guys, the ones I would laugh at, call crazy and wonder what the hell were they thinking, how could one woman keep them happy? I'm going to win this season and I'm going to win over Cammie.

The van pulls up to a house I don't know, this must be Cammie's. I'm sitting up in the front passenger seat and wishing I had jumped in the back to a seat with one available next to me. She steps off her porch pulling her large suitcase behind her. I'm getting ready to jump out and help when the back sliding door opens and Lucas jumps out first. I watch as he gives her a hug and they exchange a couple words. When he turns, our eyes meet and I'm sure mine look ready to kill him. He even has the nerve to laugh at me.

Cammie walks to the van and my breath catches, how does someone look so good this early in the morning with a pair of sweats on and a loose t-shirt with a silhouette of a bull rider on it? Her hair is in a messy twisted thing on top of her head with no makeup and she looks damn sexy. She doesn't need all of that to catch the eye of anyone, her natural beauty is enough to stop any man and have them look up at her. That's what makes Cam so different. She is comfortable with who she is and that alone is one of the reasons I find her to be the sexiest woman I've ever laid eyes on.

Climbing into the van to move all the way to the back, she says her good mornings to everyone. We have a pretty good size crew joining us for this weekend and the van is full, Cammie was the last one we needed to pick up.

There is a large rearview mirror on the front windshield, I can see almost everyone in the back seat from my seat. The large door behind me shuts and the driver pulls out onto the road. I glance into the mirror and it takes everything in me not to tear my seatbelt off and climb over everyone to get to the person the owns those eyes staring back at me. Her eyes are almost teasing me, like she purposely picked the farthest seat away from me so that I couldn't reach her. Her eyes are dancing with laughter and it's taking everything I have in me not to climb back there and prove to her that nothing is going to stand in my way when it comes to having her.

CHAPTER TWENTY-ONE

CAMMIE

It was only a couple-hour flight from Texas to Florida, not really any time to get any sleep on the plane. My seat ended up being in the same row as Lucas and Jenna and I sat at the window seat. The look of frustration on Kade's face was priceless. I have to admit, it was kind of nice seeing him go through a little misery.

Everyone with us is pretty much coupled up. Michael and Tracy are great about allowing the team members to bring along their significant others on race weekends. This weekend is no exception, everyone seems to have made the trip.

I must have dozed off somewhat because I remember the takeoff and the next thing I know I hear the flight attendant announcing that the seatbelt light would be going on shortly for the descent of our trip.

Standing around, we are all waiting for our luggage to come through the turnstile.

"Are you purposely ignoring me this morning?" His breath is hot in my ear and even though his body isn't touching mine, I can feel his heat against my back and it sends chills throughout my entire body. I ache to turn around and wrap myself around him.

"How am I ignoring you?" I try to keep my voice even but no such luck, Kade has an effect on me I can't seem to deny or hide.

"You could have sat next to me on the plane." His hand brushes the outside of my thigh.

I take a step to the side, away from his touch. I can't think straight or fast enough when he is so close. "You had two people sitting in your aisle already. One of our team members and a person no one knew, how was I supposed to sit with you? I didn't plan the assigned seating."

"Kyle could have sat next to Lucas and Jenna, all you had to do was ask," he challenges me.

Kyle and Mark are the only other two people with us this weekend that don't have someone with them. Mark's girlfriend couldn't get the time off from work and Kyle I'm sure will find someone quickly once we get settled.

My bag comes around finally. Everyone but Kade and I have their luggage, they are just waiting on us. I lean past Kade to retrieve it. "You could have offered, but you didn't." Standing with my suitcase, I pull the handle up.

Kade moves to grab his bag, slinging it over his shoulder, and before I can stop him he grabs the handle of my suitcase out of my hand and starts walking with the rest of the group through the airport.

Quickly catching up with him, I try to pull my case out of his hands, but his grip only gets tighter. "I can pull my own suitcase, Kade."

"I'm sure you can, but what kind of gentleman would I be to allow you to do that?"

The group is a little ahead of us which I'm relieved, but I also know the more I push Kade the louder he will get and the more attention he will draw to the two of us, from our group and everyone else in the airport. I know when to pick my battles. Well, sort of.

"Well, thank you." I smile the sweetest smile I can and then pick up my pace to catch up with the group in front of us, leaving him behind pulling my suitcase. I can play the games as well.

BY THE TIME we get to the hotel and everyone gets settled in their rooms, it's almost eleven. I'm waiting to hear from someone what's happening next. We all get our room keys and separate. I know the guys are all heading over to the track today to meet up with the truck and trailer and make sure everything made it through the road trip. Michael kind of cracks me up with all of that. That trailer system is the best money can buy. Once those bikes and gear are secured down there is no way they are moving, but he insists on going through everything. He checks stuff at least three times before they leave and again at least twice when we arrive. Plus, he will have the mechanics go over the bikes and make sure everything is race ready, but us women don't have to be there. I gave him my list of supplies and the check-off list to assure him I'm supply ready so by some miracle he took my word for it and decided I didn't need to go.

I've already changed clothes and have hung up the last of my clothes. Sitting on the bed, I grab my phone deciding I could text Krystal and see if any plans are being made, but a knock at my door has me throwing my phone back on my bed, that must be her or Jenna.

Opening it, I'm surprised to find Kade standing there. Michael's last comment to all of the guys was to hurry and meet him back downstairs. They were going to grab a quick bit to eat and leave.

"Kade..."

My words are cut off when he grabs both of my shoulders and pushes me back into the room, him following me, then he shuts the door with his foot. Before I know it, my back is up against the wall and Kade has claimed my lips with his. My arms instantly go around his waist and pull him tighter to me. He groans and it's so deep the vibration rumbles through his body and into mine. What was I thinking when I thought I was going to be able to keep this all professional? My body reacts to him without my consent.

His tongue quickly finds mine and his hips are pressed tightly against me. I can feel his hardness through his jeans and mine. My hands find their way under his shirt and his back muscles flex against my palms, this time the moan I hear I'm pretty sure come from me.

As quickly as it happened, it's over. His lips leave mine and a small whimper escapes through my lips from losing the feel and taste of his. His forehead is pressed hard against mine and his breathing is fast. "I can't stay away from you, no matter how hard I try to take my time and prove to you I want more than just something physical, I need to kiss you, touch you, to be inside of you."

I want to beg him to do all of that right now, but something way in the back of my mind still haunts me. Through the flowers, the card, the words, that kiss, I still see his eyes when he looked at me when he was kissing Brooke. It was almost like he was taking pleasure in punishing me while using another woman. I don't want to get into all of that with him, though, this is something I'm going to have to work out if there is ever going to be a chance for me and him.

Taking a couple deep breaths, "Didn't your dad want you guys downstairs?"

The look in his eyes has me wishing I can take my question back. Asking about his dad probably isn't the best response to what he just admitted to me.

He takes a moment and just stares down at me. It's taking everything in me not to bring his head back down to mine and continue where we just left off, but I just can't right now.

Kade nods his head and takes a couple of steps back, then

reaching for the door he opens it. Over his shoulder he tells me, "The women are waiting downstairs for you as well. I ran into Krystal and Jenna, they were on their way to come get you. I told them I would tell you they were waiting."

The door shuts before I can respond to him. Sliding down the wall, I sit down on the floor, my legs feel heavy and my knees I swear are going to buckle. My lips are swollen, I run my finger across them, I can still feel Kade's lips hard against them, his tongue searching for mine, and I feel empty without him.

Laying my head back against the wall, realization finally sinks in for me. I can't keep playing this game between us, it's not good for either party. I need to decide if I'm willing to give him another chance or just let him go altogether. I've always hated women who string guys along and I'm not all right with being one of those women.

I can't hold him being with Brooke against him, I was the one who said we were going to only have a professional relationship. He even came by one more time and tried to fix things, and again I told him no. I'm not saying he wasn't using Brooke to get back at me or make me jealous, but I need to stop using Brooke as a barrier between us, it's not like he cheated on me with her. He apologized and if I'm going to forgive him I need to forgive it all, start back with a clean slate.

My phone goes off. Getting up off the floor, my legs are still a little heavy feeling but for the most part my body has recovered from that kiss, though my need to go after him and bring him back to my room to finish what that kiss promised is still very heavy inside of me, my core still throbs a little for him.

Picking up the phone, I see a text from Krystal.

Krystal: Get down here, we have shopping to do. Boys work, we play, let's go, everyone is hungry.

Quickly I type back.

Me: On my way.

Shoving my phone in my pocket and my small wallet in the other, I hurry down to meet all the girls. They are waiting in the lobby and I know my cheeks turn red instantly when Jenna and Krystal give me that knowing look. Kade had mentioned he told them he would tell me to meet them down here, which means they know he came to my room.

"Have you forgiven my cousin yet?" Krystal wraps her arm around my waist and starts walking us out the door with the other women.

"I'm trying, trust me."

Another van is waiting out in front of the hotel for us and we all pile in, Tracey sits up front with the driver, Krystal, Jenna and I take the seat all the way to the back, which I'm thankful for because if the two of them are going to grill me about Kade, I'd rather Kade's mom not be a part of it.

"Cammie, I've never seen Kade this devoted to proving himself to anyone other than maybe on the track. I'll admit what he did between Vegas and this weekend was screwed up, but I sincerely believe he is trying to make it up to you. My cousin doesn't do mushy and somehow you have him being very soft right now."

I have nothing to say. I just give her a small smile and turn my attention out the window. Today I want to enjoy a little girl time and relax, I'll worry about what I'm going to do with Kade later. Krystal takes my hand and squeezes it, bringing my attention back to her.

"Let's go and buy the hottest bikinis we can find. What better place to shop for swimwear than shops that line the Florida beaches?"

I'm grateful she is letting the conversation go, for now at least. I know Krystal, it's not completely over, but for now we are going to enjoy our day.

. . .

THIS BATHING SUIT thing may have been a bad idea. I look at myself in the mirror with the bikini on that Krystal and Jenna talked me into buying yesterday. It's not the first time I've worn a bikini, but I'm not sure if you can call this a bathing suit, it doesn't leave much to the imagination.

Last night at dinner, Tracy told us that today was a day at the beach. Michael and Tracy has rented out a cabana down by the beach and it's going to be a day of fun for the team before the craziness of the weekend. Looking at the clock next to my bed, I realize I'm out of time and need to get downstairs. What the hell, we only live once, right? Before I can change my mind I pull on my jean shorts and loose top, grab my bag and leave, once out the door there is no going back.

Making my way down to the beach, I'm relieved when I find out I'm not the last one to show up.

"Cammie, I have a chair for you right here," Jenna grabs my attention, when I look over she is patting the chair next to her. Lucas is behind her trying to move when she does as he rubs suntan lotion over her back.

Lucas finishes his boyfriend duty and gives her a quick kiss. He walks over to me and kisses me on the cheek. "About time you finally get down here."

Pushing him away, I realize how lucky I am that he found a girl that isn't going to be jealous that we are best friends. In the past that's what usually ended relationships each of us have tried. They never understood how two people of the opposite sex could be just friends, best friends at that, without the benefit part involved as well. Jenna has never had a problem with it. She and I quickly became friends after she and Lucas started dating.

Looking around, I don't see Krystal or Cody yet, but Kade is already down here. Setting my stuff down on the chair, I can't bring myself to strip down to only my suit yet. I unsnap the button of my shorts but that's as far as I can go.

"You are wearing it, aren't you?" Jenna asks with a knowing smile on her face.

"I can't believe I let you talk me into buying it, or that I actually left my room thinking I would be all right with showing it."

"Cammie, it looks great on you and it's going to drive Kade crazy."

Driving Kade crazy isn't hard from what he has been telling me lately. "I shouldn't have let you guys talk me into this. I'm here with all the people I work with, probably not the best place to wear a suit like this. You know what? I can't, I'm going back up to change real fast. I'll be right back."

When I turn, Krystal is standing behind me, "Nope, woman up, Cammie, own that hot body you were given." She turns me back around and pushes me toward the chair.

Looking between the two girls, I realize I might as well consider this a losing battle. Live in the moment! Don't know what I'm so worried about, the suits that Jenna and Krystal are wearing are the same as mine and no one seems to be noticing them any more than usual.

Before I can change my mind again, I quickly pull my shirt up and over my head and step out of my shorts. I wait for a comment, anything, and yet nothing is said. I relax, this is all good.

I look up and realize I have definitely caught the attention of one person, Kade. He is out on the beach throwing the football around with the guys. I'll admit he doesn't look bad at all in a pair of swim shorts and no shirt. His attention is on me, even wearing sunglasses I know his eyes are on me and his jaw muscle keeps flexing, I'm going to guess his eyes are an emerald green right now. Bright and vibrant, the color they get when we are losing ourselves in each other. This is the moment I realize I don't want to push him away any longer. This might end badly and I may get hurt but that is a chance I'm willing to take again. I can't deny this pull toward him any longer.

Then it happens, the one event that sets the pace for the rest of the day. Out of nowhere the football flies through the air and right into the side of Kade's head, knocking him off balance and down into the sand. Everyone erupts into laughter, I can't hold mine back either.

"That will teach you to keep your eye on the ball!" Lucas yells. He is the one who threw the ball and I know because of the smile he has on his face. He witnessed the stare down between Kade and myself.

Kade flips him off and Lucas looks at me, giving me a wink. This is what's important. Having a great group of people around that can joke and have fun. Life doesn't always have to be so serious or all work, a little play time never hurt anyone.

CHAPTER TWENTY-TWO

KADE

The sun has gone down and the bonfire is bright and burning hot. It has cooled down and everyone is cuddled around the fire all talking about nothing important. Looking around, I can't find Cammie. I didn't see her walk away but maybe she went for a walk.

Walking out to the beach, I look both ways and see the silhouette of a woman to my left. I can't see her face from here, but I'm pretty sure it's Cammie. Making my way over to her, I stand behind her for a bit and just watch her. She looks deep in thought. Her arms are wrapped around herself, trying to keep the chill away. I see her body shiver and I can't stay away any longer.

Walking up close behind her, I wrap my arms around her. She jumps and tries to pull away, but I tighten my hold on her and without me having to say a word she relaxes in my arms.

"Kade, you scared me." She surprises me even more when her head falls back and relaxes against my chest.

"Sorry, you looked cold. Why are you out here alone?"

She shrugs her shoulders, "Just out here listening to the waves, I love the sound of the ocean and at night when you can't really see the waves in front of you, it holds a little mystery to it. Plus, I was thinking."

"Care to share?"

She is silent for a moment and I give her that time. I'm all right with just holding her right now. It's nice not having her pull away from me. Sure, our fire we share when things are sexual is intense and I dream every night of having that with her again, but this is something I've never really experienced before. It's light, but warm. That need to have her is always there but right now there is something else and I'm liking that just as much.

"I can't fight this pull between us anymore," her voice is low, "I don't want to fight it anymore either."

I'm not sure what is going to come next but I'm pretty sure she can feel my heart beating against the back of her head through my chest.

Her head comes up off my chest and she steps out of my embrace. My heart stops, and I swear I can't take a solid breath. She turns and looks right up into my eyes. I want to wrap my arms around her again, pull her tight to me and beg her to give me another chance, but instead my arms stay to my side and I just wait for her to finish.

She stares up at me for a moment and for once I can't get a handle on what she might be thinking. Finally, she takes a step closer to me and places her hand against my chest above my heart. It begins to beat again with her touch.

Her other hand rests against my cheek. "I'm all yours, Kade," that hand moves to the back of my head and she pulls me down to her until our lips touch.

My arms instantly go around her pulling her to me, not rough, but closer. The kiss isn't about desire or lust. It's soft and promises so much more than sex. This is the moment I realize, I don't just have feelings for Cammie, I'm pretty sure I'm falling in love with her.

I'm not sure how long we stand here, the waves are running over our feet and up our legs, it's cold, but I can't break this moment between us. She surprises me even more when she wraps an arm around my waist and pulls me tight to her, then deepens the kiss, her tongue now searching for mine. It takes my body only seconds to realize what she is asking for.

"Kade, I can't deny myself any longer, I need you, please."

Cammie begging is the sexiest thing I've ever heard. "We can walk back to the hotel."

Her lips are against my neck and I can feel her head shake no. That's all it takes. Looking around, I notice a rock cove. Pulling away from those lips on my body is hard, but the reward of what is to come gets my feet moving. Grabbing her hand I all but pull her, praying that once we get behind the rocks someone else hasn't already had the same idea.

Cammie laughs behind me as I basically run. Rounding the corner, I don't see another person anywhere. I don't really have much time to worry about it, and Cammie doesn't seem to care if there is or isn't.

Before I know it I'm pressed against the rocks and they start to bite into my back, but Cammie already has my shirt up and her lips and tongue on my chest. That takes away any discomfort from the rocks behind me.

Cammie in control is fire and I'm more than happy to allow her to take the lead right now. Her teeth nip at both my nipples and my knees about buckle. I'm thankful for swim shorts and how roomy they are because every time her teeth pull on one nipple I become just a little harder. My head falls back against the rock as I allow her full access to whatever she wants to do with my body. I feel her fingers sink in under the band of my shorts and my breath hitches waiting for what she wants next. Before I know it she is on her knees in front of me, her tongue running over my abs as her hands push my shorts down over my legs and around my feet.

Pulling back, I watch as she looks me over, her eyes feasting on my hardness in front of her. With a tip of her finger she smears the bead of moisture around the tip of me and I have to lock my knees to keep from falling to the ground. There is no way I'm going to not let her finish what she has started.

Her eyes look up at me, ice blue, my favorite color. Her eyes never leave mine as she slowly leans forward. I watch as her tongue lightly runs over the tip, I harden even more, which I wasn't aware was even possible. With her eyes locked to mine, her tongue runs down and then slowly back up. Just when I'm pretty sure I'm going to lose myself, she takes me all the way into her mouth, her eyes never leaving mine.

I watch as she sucks me in as far as she can and then pulls back just until her tongue is playing with the tip. She smiles and then repeats.

Her never breaking eye contact with me as she sucks me deep inside of her mouth has to be one of the sexiest things I've ever witnessed, but I can't hold my release much longer and I need to be deep inside of her when it happens.

I start to slide down to the sand with her, this makes her have to release me from her mouth. She pouts a little and that almost does it right there. "Don't pout, Cam, I've never experienced anything sexier than you sucking me and watching me as you just did, but I need to be so deep inside of you right now it hurts."

She surprises me when she stands up. I'm about to protest until I see what her intentions are. She pulls her shirt up and over her head, letting it fall to the ground and her shorts follow quickly behind. She reaches behind her back to remove her bikini top and that's where I have to stop her.

"I have fantasized about stripping you out of this suit all day, please don't deny me of it now."

Her hands drop from the tie at her back and she stands there in front of me waiting. I start by running a hand up each leg together. I loop my fingers into the strings holding her bottoms on and slowly pull them down her legs. Holding onto my shoulder, she steps out of them, now only standing in front of me in just the top. As bad as I want to be very deep inside of her there is nothing that is going to stop me from tasting her first. Spreading her legs just enough so that I can get between them, I decide taking anything slow right now isn't going to happen. Slow can be later, I need to taste her now.

Bending forward, I thrust my tongue into her very wet core. Her hands clutch my hair tightly and she bends forward, a moan escaping from her. My hands are at her backside and I push her into me, my tongue pushing as far as I can inside of her.

"Kade, please." Her legs start to shake. I haven't had enough, but I will have to come back to that later. With my hands on her waist, I lie back and pull her down to straddle me. As she slides down she takes me deep inside of her and instantly begins to grind against me. Her top is still on and I want to see her breasts bounce with her movement. Sitting up, I quickly pull it up and over her head, taking one breast fully into my mouth, biting onto the nipple. She tightens around me.

"I need you to ride me hard, Cam."

With her hands on my chest she pushes me back down into the sand. She sits up and braces her hands behind her on my legs, thrusting her hips forward and taking me even deeper inside of her. Her hips start moving in a circular motion and I've never felt anything like it. Her head falls back and her hair brushes my legs. I'm so close and so is she, with each thrust I can feel her tighten a little more. Her head comes back up and her eyes lock with mine. Her hand comes around and with her own fingers she reaches down and circles her sensitive bud. Her eyes I swear are pure white and watching her massage herself is all I can take. With my hands on her hips, I pull her hard down onto me a couple of times and that's all it takes. Her body convulses around me, pulling me deeper and deeper as I fill her with my release. I'm not sure which of us is louder or if anyone hears us, but I really don't care either.

Cammie is now draped across me, her head resting on my chest. "We should probably get dressed before someone starts looking for us."

Now she is worried about someone finding us? She just stood here, sucking me deep into her mouth and now she is worried. I have to laugh, that's my girl. Once in the moment she is a warrior of passion and couldn't care less about what's going on around her, it's only me and her. The building could be falling around us and she wouldn't even hesitate or stop. Once everything has cooled and she is satisfied, my little worrier comes back and she worries about everyone else and that we may get caught.

"Why are you laughing at me?" She pushes herself away from me and slaps my chest before she gets to her feet and starts collecting her discarded clothes. I watch as she shakes the sand off of them and then starts to put them back on.

Before I can get up my shorts are thrown at me. "Get up and get dressed," and there is the bossy side of my girl.

Quickly standing up, I pull my shorts back on and find my t-shirt. "How is it you worry now about us being caught, but not earlier when I was between your legs?"

Even though it's dark out I can see the redness of embarrassment spread over her cheeks. She starts to look around us.

Wrapping my arms around her waist, I pull her tight to me. "Calm down, Cam, no one is around." I watch as she tries to pull her hair onto the top of her head and wrap a rubber band that she had around her wrist around it, containing it all there.

"We should probably head back to everyone else, I'm sure they are wondering where we are." She tries to pull out of my arms, but I only tighten them around her.

"We need to talk. We kind of jumped right into the fun stuff first. Cammie, I'm taking what you said earlier and what just happened here in the sand as you telling me you are going to give me another chance?"

"I've tried, Kade. Tried so hard to make my heart agree with my head. Am I a hundred percent sure this a good idea? No. But I can't listen to just my head. I have always been someone who believed in following the heart. I'm just hoping I'm doing the right thing for the both of us."

Bringing my lips down to hers, I claim them in a soft kiss. No passion, just understanding. "I can't tell you what's going to happen between the two of us. I can tell you that I'm sure I'm going to mess up, more than a couple times. This is going to be all new to me. Just be patient and we will make this work. I'm not going to hide this, Cammie, I'm going to kiss you when I want, I'm going to hold your hand when we walk around, I'm not going to tip-toe around our relationship."

"I know and I'm okay with that."

"All right, well, let's get back to everyone, because I'm good with saying goodnight and heading back to one of our rooms. I haven't had enough of you yet and I plan to spend the rest of the evening making up for the last month."

CHAPTER TWENTY-THREE

CAMMIE

There is something different in Kade today and the way he is riding. It looks effortless, like he is almost gliding around the track. His body isn't tense, his arms and legs pump evenly with the bike. He is riding with a confidence I didn't see in the last set of races in Vegas.

Jenna is sitting next to me cheering him on every time he comes around and starts a new lap, but I'm mesmerized and can only watch. The riders are visible throughout most of the track. There are only two spots they dip out of sight from where I'm sitting right now and my eyes move right to the spot where they come back into sight and I find that I hold my breath every time until I see him again, hoping he hasn't lost the first place spot, which isn't necessary. He has a good lead on everyone.

"He is going to get first today." Jenna grabs onto my arm, jumping up and down.

There it is, the checkered flag, and just like that the race is over. Jenna grabs my hand and starts pulling me through the bleachers to go and meet back with the team.

As we are walking back over to our staging area, Kade is just coming around the corner. I watch as Michael and Kade speak to a couple of staff members. The bike gets handed off by Lucas for inspection and the spectators take that opportunity to crowd around and ask for autographs. He is being polite and signing everything from posters, helmets, jerseys and yes, even some chests of women who ask but he keeps it very professional as his dad tries to move him through the crowd and finally he disappears into the trailer.

Jenna and I walk slowly behind the crowd and wait for them to move on.

"You go check on your rider, I'm going to wait for Lucas to get back in the trailer." Jenna walks away before I can say anything.

Entering the trailer, I don't see Kade. "Kade, where did you go?"

He pokes his head out from my room. "I'm patiently waiting for you in here."

Before I can step over the doorway, his arm loops around my waist, pulling me inside. His lips hungrily find mine and I hear the door slam shut, then I'm turned and pushed up against the door, Kade's hands going everywhere.

Laughing, I try to take a large breath of air into my lungs. "This is some kind of adrenaline rush. Someone can walk into the trailer, Kade, this place has the thinnest walls ever."

"Right now I don't care who walks in, I want you bent over that table and me very, very deep inside of you."

Before I can respond, he is turning me away from the wall and him. My back to him now, his hands come around and unbutton my jeans, and instantly one of his fingers is deep inside my very wet and heated center.

"Cam, you are already so wet." He pushes his finger deep inside of me and I arch to push it deeper. Now I don't give a damn who walks in and what they might hear.

Pulling his finger from me, I gasp at how empty I feel and want to beg him for more. Before I can say anything he pushes my pants and panties down over my legs to my feet. With his hand on my back, he pushes me down over the table.

"Cam, I need you to spread your legs farther apart," he whispers in my ear.

Kicking off my shoes, I maneuver one leg out of my pants and that allows me to spread my legs more for him. I feel his lips on one cheek and then the other. "This is going to be fast, Cam. I'm sorry, I just need to be inside of you."

"Please, Kade," I push myself back against him and can feel how hard he is. I'm ready and wanting it just as fast.

I hear him unzip his pants and the sound of them being pushed down his legs. His hands are on my hips and with one thrust he is deep inside of me. I arch off the table and push myself into him, hoping to get him even deeper.

I let him have control and go along for the ride, it doesn't take long before I find my release and I hear my own moan fill the room.

"Damn, that feels good, pull me in deeper, Cam." I feel my body pull him in deeper and deeper with each pulse. Then he finally releases and his body goes tight up against mine.

"I'm going to have no problem winning this series if that's going to be my prize." Kade's breathing is still labored but full of life.

"Kade, are you still in here?" Michael's voice echoes through the trailer.

"Yep, just in here getting worked out by Cammie, be out in a minute."

I try to twist my upper body around to slap him from the side, but his body is still pressed into my back and he is still deep inside of me. Nothing like talking to a man's father in this position.

"All right, try to be out in five." Michael is standing at the door now and I can feel my body heat up from embarrassment. Now I just pray he doesn't try and come in. How Kade can sound so casual right now is beyond me.

"Got it, almost done." Turning my head, I look up at Kade the best I can. I try to stand up but he keeps a hand at my back. "Easy, hon, don't want you hurting either one of us." He pulls out slowly and I have to stop a moan that is building inside.

"I'm good to go for another round if you are?" Kade's voice is light and playful behind me.

"No, I'm not going to have your dad coming in and talking through the door again, or worse yet, coming into the room checking on you and how your workout is going." I push away from him and quickly redress.

"You are cute when you are embarrassed." Kade tries to wrap his arms around my waist and pull me into him again but I manage to dance away from him.

"And nothing embarrasses you, so stop teasing me and get out there and see what your dad wants." I open the door and push him out.

He turns quickly on me. "One more kiss and I promise you I'll leave."

How do I deny that? Grabbing him at the back of the head, I claim his lips with mine. It's hard and still holds a lot of heat behind it, but I find the ability to push away from him and send him out of the trailer before we become lost in each other once again.

THE REST of the weekend flies by. Both Cody and Kade take first place in each of their divisions. The whole team goes out for a celebration dinner Sunday night and Kade and I celebrate on our own through the rest of the night. This trip couldn't have gone any better!

The next month is no different. Kade is sitting very comfortable in the point standings to take first this season, which seems to put everyone on the team in a very good mood. The last race is this weekend and victory for the team has everyone pretty pumped up for the last race of the series. Michael isn't going easy on the boys, they practice longer hours and harder than I have seen them do the last couple of months, but no one complains. I'm just busy with sore muscles and keeping both boys in the best shape I can.

My phone starts going off in my office. Walking inside, I sit down and pick it up, seeing it's Sam. "Hey, how is everything going?"

"I miss you terribly and I think when this whole race thing is over, you need to come up and visit. I can use a little Cammie time."

"I know, hun, I don't like us being this far apart. This season has its last race this weekend and then we have a couple months before the next season starts, so I will try to get up there and visit you."

We went from being roommates for three years, seeing each other every day and being there for each other, to living almost fifteen thousand miles away from each other. "How are you doing?"

"Everything is working itself out over here, I called to hear about how things down there are going. You have heard of nothing else but my situation up here every time we talk, it's your turn. Last time we chatted you were dating a pretty hot rider that you work with, how is all of that going?"

"Surprisingly, really well."

"So you are trading your tight pants, cowboy boots and hat-wearing kind of guy for a dirt bike racer, huh?"

"I know, can you believe it?" Sometimes I don't even believe it. I'm a country girl who has always been attracted to bull riders and cowboys, I don't even think Kade has ever been on a horse.

Kade walks into the training center looking freshly showered.

Looking up at the clock, I'm a little surprised, it's only a little after one. Holding up a finger, I signal to give me a minute. He nods and props himself against the doorframe of my office.

"Sam, I hate to cut this short, I miss you tons and I promise I will try to make it up there to see you, but work is calling and I need to go."

"All right, but I'm expecting a call back soon. I didn't get any good details on this guy."

Kade's eyebrows lift up and he gets one of his cocky smiles on his face, he must be able to hear Sam over the phone.

"I promise to call you back soon. I know I'm pretty far away and limited to what I can do, but know if you need me I'm only a flight away. I will be on the first plane up there."

"I know and that's why I love you. Talk soon." Sam hangs up before I can say anything else.

Kade walks over and sits on my desk in front of me, "Was that your friend from college?"

Standing up, I settle myself between his legs and wrap my arms around his neck, gently kissing him on the lips.

We have agreed that we need to keep control of ourselves while here at the center. I can't keep count of the times we have had someone almost walk in on us. Not that I expect any of them not to know what we were doing, I can't keep guilty off my face Kade tells me, but no one has said anything and Kade knows how important it is to me to keep things in the work environment professional.

"Yes, that was Sam, I promised to go up and see her in between the race seasons."

"Maybe I'll come with you. I mean if she wants good details, what's better than meeting me in person, right?"

"You would want to come with me?" I have to admit I am a little surprised, not sure why, but all the same I am.

"Sure, I would like to meet her, she sounds important to you."

"Next to you and Lucas, she is right there with you guys. Are you guys already done for the day?" I run my fingers through his wet hair.

"Yep, Dad has some meeting to go to, so he called an early day. What are your plans for the day?"

"I was going to go home and ride my horse for a while today after work, I've been neglecting him a little lately, it seems another man is taking up a lot of my time."

Kade pulls me in tight to him and kisses my neck, "I have no idea who that could be." His lips move over my neck and it tickles.

Pushing him away is hard, but not here. "Do you want to come riding with me?"

I just mentioned to Sam I wasn't sure if Kade had ever been on a horse, why not find out now?

"Cam, I've never been on a horse. People get hurt on those things."

"Those things," I repeat, laughing. "You ride dirt bikes for heaven's sake. I've watched you jump and the tricks you do on that thing and you are worried about getting on a horse?"

"I have control over the bike, no one can control an animal. You may think you have control, but then something happens. I know what my bike is going to do. If I crash it's because I did something wrong."

"So you are saying you won't get on a horse?"

"That's exactly what I'm telling you."

I have to say I'm a little surprised. There is something that may scare Kade. "All right, well how about this. Why don't you bring your bike to the house, and you can ride your bike while I ride my horse?"

"No offense, but that doesn't even sound fun. You would never be able to keep up and I'd be stopping all the time to wait for you."

"You are joking, right?" I look at him in disbelief. From the look he is giving me he isn't kidding, "Kade, I will have no problem keeping up with you, it may be the other way around. I may have to wait for you."

"Are you challenging me to a race?" Kade's eyes beam with the challenge.

"Absolutely, Zodiac and I are going to show you what real riding is."

In one fast motion, his arms wraps around me and he pulls me in tight, his lips claiming mine with a hunger that is hard to deny, but again we are at work and I need to stop both of us. Pulling back is hard.

"You have no idea how much I want you right now, but later. First, I'm going to kick your butt in this race, because I've never been a gentleman when it comes to a challenge. I won't let you win. But, after the race, you are coming home with me tonight."

Since I'm still living at home, we stay most of the time at Kade's house. I've been thinking it's time for me to find an apartment because even though I'm old enough to have my own life without explaining what and where I'm going, I still feel like an awkward teenager when I do come home and hope my parents don't ask a lot of questions. They never have but it's still weird.

I grind my hips into his and can feel his hardness through his jeans. I feel his breath hitch inside his chest against mine, his arm tightens around my waist pulling me in tighter to him, and his eyes become hooded.

"You have to win first, don't be so sure you get to claim the prize," I whisper against his lips.

Kade's lips brush mine lightly, and then he smiles, "Just to let you know I really like this side of you, it's damn sexy on you."

"Pack a small bag for the night." She pulls from my embrace.

"Why?" I'm confused. We don't stay the night at her parents' house, they don't allow it and I'm perfectly all right with it.

CHAPTER TWENTY-FOUR

KADE

Pulling up to Cammie's house, I pull around to the back and park near the barn. I've been back here a couple times with her while she was feeding the six horses they have on the property, but never have I seen her ride. She is in the round pin when I pull up, sitting tall and proud on top of a very large black and white horse. I kill the engine of my truck and just sit and watch her for a moment.

I realize I've never asked her much about all of this. I figured she knew how to ride, who would have horses and not ride them, but I'm feeling like an ass hat right now for never being more interested in her likes and hobbies. Everything around the two of us as a couple is racing. She even asked to try and ride my bike once, did pretty good for someone who had never rode one before.

Watching her now, though, it's beautiful! I know nothing about horses, or how to ride one, but she looks like she and the horse are in rhythm together. The way both of their bodies move in motion with each other is amazing to watch. Her petite, the horse all power, and she looks very comfortable.

When she comes around her eyes look up and her smile beams as she waves at me. I watch has she pulls the horse to a stop and throws her leg over to climb down the large animal. When she stands on the ground, she looks child-sized next to the giant.

As she walks toward me, I get out of the truck and meet her at the back of it.

"Are you having second thoughts?" She walks up and gives me a small kiss.

She has on a pair of jeans and a grey tank top, boots and her cowboy hat. So simple and so beautiful. "Not on your life." I point over to her horse, "I'm assuming that is your horse?"

Looking over her shoulder she nods, when she looks back at me there is pride in her eyes, "Yep, that's Zodiac."

"He is amazing, and huge."

She laughs, "Yes, he isn't easy to miss, but very gentle. Well, let's get going," she lifts the handle of the tailgate and pulls it down, pulling the ramp out.

"Are you in a hurry to lose?" I jump into the back of the truck and start loosening up the tie downs on the bike.

She just shakes her head and laughs, a sound that I'm quickly falling in love with. "You are on my track now. You don't have to be the fastest to win a race, just the quickest to react, but for now you can believe you are going to win."

She drops the ramp down on the gate and in place for me to push the bike back and out of the truck, then walks away and back to her horse. As I'm putting on my gear I watch as she makes some adjustments to the saddle and rubs the horse's legs down. With ease she pulls her leg up and puts a foot in the stirrup and then pulls herself up into the saddle like the horse isn't double her height.

She rides over to me and waits. Grabbing my helmet, I walk over and start up the bike. "All right, so where are we going?"

She points straight ahead of her, "About two miles right ahead of us is a lake that we have on the property, it will be a straight shot from here. I'll warn you, we have some fallen trees and you will have to maneuver over some terrain, but you can't miss the lake. First one there I would say is the winner."

"Sounds fun, you say when, I'll see you at the lake." Smiling, I shove my helmet on my head and strap it on. I rev up the bike a couple of times and the horse next to me doesn't even flinch. His attention is in front of him and I can see a shiver run through his body, he is anticipating her command to go.

Looking over, I see her hand come up. She puts three fingers up and I nod my understanding. She counts down and then takes off, I quickly overtake her and fire off down the straightaway. I warned her I wasn't going to just let her win.

Just as quick as we start I'm finding myself hitting me brakes as I come onto the more vegetative part of her property. I quickly scan the area for the best route for me to take with the bike, this is going to slow me down drastically. Before I know it I spot a large black mass off to my right, when I look over its Cammie and Zodiac running through like there is nothing in their way. I turn my head to look over at her just as the horse sails through the air and over a fallen tree, landing sure-footed like it was a tiny twig on the ground.

There are a couple small trails, I pick the one to my left and start to pick up speed. We now seem to be racing side by side of each other. I can no longer see her and I look to my right to see where she went. Mistake! I feel my tire catch onto something and before I know it my bike is stopping and I'm flying over the handle bars, seconds later followed by the feel of the hard ground and me coming in contact with each other. I roll, hoping to keep from majorly injuring something.

I lie for a second without moving, taking a couple deep breaths and waiting for the feel of any pain after the adrenaline slows down. I'm sure I'll be sore but other than that I'm not feeling anything that may be broken. Starting to sit up, my hands sink down a little, mud! This may have been my saving grace.

Sitting up, I run my gloved hands over my pants before bringing them up to unstrap my helmet. I pull it off just in time to hear Cammie, "Whoa, Zodiac."

I look up and see her jump off the horse before he comes to a complete stop.

"Kade, Kade!" She runs over to me and basically slides in the mud the last couple feet, landing on her knees next to me.

"I'm all right, Cam." Her hands are everywhere, feeling for injury.

"Take your shirt off, I want to check your back and ribs," she demands as her hands continue to work over my legs.

I don't even attempt to calm her down, I see the fear in her eyes. She isn't going to be happy until she checks for herself so I pull my gloves off and then pull my shirt up and over my head. Her hands expertly run over my back and down my ribs. Finally, I hear her exhale a very deep breath and she sits back on her heels.

"Nothing seems to be broken."

"I told you I was all right."

"What the heck happened? One minute you are racing past me, the next your bike is stopping and you are not."

"I looked over to get a glimpse of you, just making sure that beast hadn't thrown you and well, I should have known better than to take my eyes off terrain like this. I didn't see the rock but my bike felt it. Next think I know I'm in the mud."

Cammie climbs onto my lap, straddling me and wraps her arms around my neck, holding me tight against her in a hug. "I was so scared."

I hold her for a moment while her breathing evens out. Pulling back, I get her to look at me. "Cam, this isn't the first time and probably not the last time I'll crash."

"I know that, but it's the first time I've watched you crash."

There is something in her eyes, something I haven't seen before, something over the fear. My heart stops and I think this moment is when we both realize this thing between us is more than we thought. Feelings that I know I have never felt before. Would I stamp the word onto it for sure, yes I would, but it doesn't seem either of us are ready to speak them out loud. Her eyes are saying everything that neither of us can put to words just yet.

Her lips find mine and it's the final confirmation for both of us. This kiss isn't about the heat, the passion, or the need we have for each other, it's about the unspoken words.

When the kiss ends we are forehead to forehead and staring at each other. There is a pulse between us, or more like a single strong heartbeat.

"Kade...?"

"I know, Cam. Trust me, I feel it, too."

Another couple of seconds pass and then Cammie blinks like she is coming out of a trance. "Let's see what kind of damage is done to the bike. We aren't far from the lake, we can walk from here if it isn't running."

She springs up from the mud and starts back in the direction of where my bike is laying. I get up a little slower just to make sure everything is moving correctly. Reaching her side, she is just standing there with her hands on her hips and looking down at my bike. "Not sure if it's running, but I'm thinking it's safe to assume that by the bend in that tire you won't be riding it the rest of the way."

Standing the bike up, it's not only the tire but the handle bars are bent as well. "Walking it is."

IT TAKES us about twenty minutes to reach the clearing, Cammie walks next to me leading Zodiac. When it opens up I'm surprised by what I see. It's a lake, with a dock going out to it, a gazebo set up with a picnic table and chairs, and the biggest surprise is the little shed looking building with a porch around it.

"Not what I was expecting when you said a lake, this is all set up out here."

"Growing up we had a lot of parties out here, ones my parents know about and some that they don't. We used to come out here as a family and just spend the weekends, that's why dad built that little house there. It just one large room, with a bed, a sink and a wood-burning stove. We used to cook over the fire pit over there," she points to the large pit in front of the building, it has benches all around it that look to be made out of logs.

Following Cammie over to the building, I prop my bike against the side of the small shack. She unties a bag from her saddle that I have just now noticed. "What's all of that?"

She smiles, "Dinner."

She heads to the shack, I follow her smiling. My girl set this all up. That's what the comment about bringing an overnight bag was all about, we are staying here tonight.

She looks over her shoulder just before entering through the door. "We are the only two out here tonight.

I like this side of Cammie. We are usually at work, or just hanging out at my house after we go out to dinner or something. This is a sexy side of her that I'm regretting not getting to know earlier.

Following her inside, it's small but enough room for at least four to sleep. There is a double bed against one wall and a set of bunk beds against the opposite. A stove in one corner and a sink against the wall.

Cammie sets down the bag, I can't stay away from her any longer. Walking up behind her, I grab her tank top and lift it up and over her head. She doesn't stop me, or ask what I'm doing, she just stands there and awaits my next move. I unclasp her bra and let it fall over her arms. Bringing my arms around, I cup a breast in each of my hands. Her head falls to one side and my lips trail small kisses from her shoulder, up her neck to her ear.

"I wish I could explain to you what is going on inside of me right now, but I know I can show you."

She turns in my arms and looks me over, "Right now I think we need to get you cleaned off." She grabs the bottom of my shirt and pulls it up and over my head, "Why don't you get those boots off and meet me outside?"

Before I can say anything she is out the door. I most definitely like the playful Cammie. I don't want to take my dirty boots off here in the room, shouldn't have even walked in here with them, so I step out onto the porch. Standing out on the dock is a now naked Cammie. Bending over, I unbuckle my boots and try to quickly pull them off, losing my balance and almost falling over. I hear Cammie's laughter from across the way.

Once I have managed to get out of my clothes I run in the direction of the dock. Before I can reach her, she runs and jumps off the end and into the water. I follow in right after her.

Surfacing only inches away from her, I wrap my arms around her waist and pull her naked body against mine.

Her arms go around the neck, together we kick to keep ourselves above water.

"I thought that you might need a night of fun and relaxation before this weekend's race. I thought about when I was the most relaxed and this place came to mind. Thought we could have a little fun and alone time before the craziness of the final races. From what Lucas tells me, it's going to be a very busy weekend. I even chatted with your dad and asked for tomorrow off for the both of us, so we are in no hurry to get back tomorrow, although he may not be very happy about the now broken bike."

She is just full of surprises tonight. Her asking to have a day off together I'm sure wasn't easy for her, she doesn't like to bring a lot of attention to our relationship with work. She hasn't figured it out yet, but my parents adore her, she has tamed their wild son.

"It's all an easy fix. Dad won't even have to know what

happened. He would lecture me more on not paying attention than anything."

Cammie laughs and pushes herself out of my arms and swims back to the edge. I catch up with her just as she gets out. Grabbing her once again, I bring her down to the thick grass around the edge of the lake.

Instantly her arms go around my neck and her lips find mine. We aren't going anywhere until I get to be inside of her at least once first. Trailing kisses down her neck, her chest, I then find one breast begging me for some attention. I circle her tight nipple a couple of times with my tongue and then suck it hard into my mouth. Cammie moans and arches her back, her hands in my hair pushing me harder to her.

Her body speaks to me, she needs no words to tell me what she wants. I need her just as much as she needs me right now.

Positioning myself above her, she spreads her legs wider, the tip of my hardness finds her very hot and ready core. I can't hold back, with one thrust I'm deep inside of her. I stay still for a moment, enjoying the feeling of her surrounding me.

"Kade, please move." Her nails scratch down my back.

Pulling almost all the way out of her, I give her a moment and then thrust forward again, even deeper this time. Her nails dig harder into my back. There will be marks and I'm all right with that, it will be a reminder of this moment.

"Again," she says, breathless.

That's my undoing, no longer able to take this slow, I thrust into her over and over, faster each time. Her legs wrap around my waist, her whimpers become moans, her moans turn into my name and that's when I feel her release as it surrounds me, pulling me deeper and deeper with each pulse. It doesn't take long for mine to follow.

CHAPTER TWENTY-FIVE

CAMMIE

The sun coming through the window heats the little room up fast this morning. Between that and Kade curved around me, it's almost too much. He looks really young when he is sleeping. There is no cocky grin on his face, no mischief in his eyes, his jaw isn't flexing, which I think now he knows what it does to me and does it all the time. My hand is pressed against his chest between us and I can feel the steady rhythm of his heartbeat. I flex my fingers slightly, feeling the heat of his skin. Leaning forward, I brush a light kiss just above my hand. I'm falling in love with this man and it's scaring me to death. I don't think I've actually been in love before.

Yesterday when I watched him fly over the handle bars of his bike, my heart stopped. I knew there was nothing I could do but watch, I felt helpless and when he didn't move right away after he landed, I realized I stopped breathing. I was off Zodiac and running in a full sprint, but I felt like he was miles away from me and I couldn't get over to him fast enough. That's when I realized I couldn't lose him or I would be shattered. Sitting there with him after checking for anything broken, I realized I was in love with him, without a question.

"Are you all right?" Kade's husky voice brings me out of my thoughts and that's when I feel the tear running down my cheek.

Nodding, I keep my face down toward his chest. I don't want him to see me crying.

"Hey, what's going on?" he asks as he tries to push back to look down at me.

"Nothing." I try to keep my face down, but he isn't having any of it. His finger goes under my chin and lightly pushes my face up to look at him.

"Are you crying?" He gently runs his thumb over my cheek, concern filing his eyes.

"It's nothing, I'm fine." I try to push away from him, but his arms tighten around me.

"Cam, you don't cry over nothing."

I take a deep breath and avert my eyes back to his chest. "I was thinking about your accident yesterday." My voice is just a little above a whisper, I know he is going to think I'm being over sensitive, he is fine and here I am worrying about it.

He kisses me on the forehead, "Cam, I'm all right."

"I know. It just scared me to watch you being thrown from the bike. I think it brought the reality of what might happen to you while you are racing."

"Have you seen that beast outside that you ride? It can just as easily happen to you."

"Zodiac would never throw me, he would go down before I did and do whatever he could to make sure I got as little injury as possible. He is a gentle giant."

"That may be, but horses spook, or misplace a footing, it's no different than me being on the bike."

I get what he is saying, but it isn't making me feel any better at the moment. The vision of him flying off the bike is very fresh in my mind.

"Speaking of my bike, how are we going to get it back to the house?"

"I'll ride back on Zodiac and grab your truck and drive it over. I would say you can ride with me, but you don't seem very excited about getting on a horse."

"How are you going to bring my truck through all of that terrain?"

I know my smile is a guilty one. "Through the dirt road that goes between here and the house."

"A dirt road?" He is looking at me with disbelief in his eyes.

"I had to even out the chances of running against you. Zodiac is lightning when he is in a full run, but I've watched you ride that bike, you have no fear of opening it all the way up. I had to even out the race track."

"Woman, you are going to be my undoing, I swear."

THE LAST RACE is in Missouri. We flew in yesterday morning and this morning starts all the activities for the last race of the season. The boys are at a riders' signing event this afternoon, everyone gets checked in this morning and tonight is a dinner for all of the teams. Kade is being pulled in every which direction for interviews and sponsors. I just hang back with Lucas.

"This place is packed this weekend." I look around at all trailers and motorhomes. This race seems to be at least triple the size of the rest we have attended.

"This is the final weekend, it's always crazy. Today is all the interviews and promo photoshoots. Fan signings, that kind of stuff. Once the heats start tomorrow, there won't be any contact with the riders and the fans. Once the race ends on Sunday, the rest of the night is a big party." Lucas turns his attention from the crowd in front of us to me, "I see we are sharing a room this weekend."

It isn't a question, it is a fact. I feel my cheeks turn a couple of shades of red. "Why do you sound surprised? It's not like we just started seeing each other."

"We all knew it was going to take one strong woman to switch the player in Kade, when I suggested you for this job I would have never thought you would have been that woman. It's actually one of the reasons I thought you would be perfect for this job, you are all country, your men included, never would I have guessed you would have fallen for a motocross rider."

Looking back to the crowds I spot Kade, he is talking to a reporter with ten other mics shoved in his face as he answers question after question. He looks relaxed and in his element. "Trust me, I'm just as surprised as all of you."

"You love him, don't you?"

Surprised, I swing my attention back to my best friend. He is giving me that no bullshit look. He is my best friend and he knows me better than anyone, probably even Sam. I just nod, the words aren't ready to pass through my lips just yet.

"Have you told him?"

Shaking my head no, I take a couple deep breaths to slow down my racing heart.

"Are you going to tell him?" Lucas is pushing now.

Again, I shake my head no.

"Cammie, what are you waiting for?"

"What if it pushes him away? I don't think he is ready for those words yet, I'm not sure if I'm ready for that yet. I can't even say the words out loud, Lucas, that tells me it isn't the right time."

Lucas wraps an arm around my shoulder and pulls me into his side. "He'd be crazy to run from you."

Wrapping my arms around his waist, I hug Lucas as I stand

there and watch Kade in his world. After this weekend he will be number one, I couldn't be prouder of him.

DINNER IS NICE, just a big barbeque out under the stars, music and lots of people. Again Kade is pulled around from one sponsor to the other by his father. He sits down with me for about ten minutes while he tries to shovel some food down, but his dad finds him pretty quickly, pulling him to meet another sponsor yet again.

Looking out toward the track, the lights catch my attention. Looking over my shoulder, Kade seems to be in a pretty serious conversation with some guy so I decide to take a walk, get away from all the noise for a few minutes.

Walking up to the edge of the track, I just look around. It looks so calm, almost peaceful when there aren't twenty bikes tearing around each of the corners throwing up dirt. Ducking under the fence, I walk out onto the dirt track. Looking down from this angle is intimidating. I can't really see over the next mound, or around the curve, a rider is basically blind throughout some of this race, yet they speed around it without any fear of what may be around the corner. This is what makes the sport so dangerous, the unknown around each corner, over each hill. There can be a rider down and no one would know until that flag goes up to slow the race down. It's not just the crashing you have to fear, but the chance of a rider coming around or landing on top of you while you are down, your race can end in seconds.

"Quick reflexes," the deep voice comes from behind me, right before the arms circle around my waist and pull me up tight against his chest.

I instantly relax against him, resting my hands over his, "What about quick reflexes?"

"You are wondering how we manage to miss a crash."

"How do you know that?"

"Because when I walked up, you were standing on your tippy toes trying to see over the hill and you had a look on your face that was confused yet a little terrified. I've told you a couple of times, Cam, your eyes say a lot about what you are thinking."

"It seems so much bigger out here than when you sit in the stands and watch, so many blind curves and jumps."

"That's why we have sighting laps, so we can familiarize ourselves with the course." He grabs my hand and we start walking along the track.

"Shouldn't you be back with the others? How did you even know where I was?"

"I'm sorry I haven't been with you a lot today..."

"Kade, please don't apologize, I've been fine. This is your day, this is stuff you need to do. I've enjoyed watching actually. You look happy in this element, relaxed."

"I'll be honest, it's all a little exhausting. When Lucas told me he saw you walk out this way I thought what a great way to get away from it all for a minute. Even outside it can become a little stuffy, plus there is one thing I have always wanted to do out on the track that I've never done and it being with you on this weekend seems right."

He stops and I look over at him with a questioning look, but my breath catches the instant I look at him. I know that look, I know those eyes and that smile.

"Out here?" I look around and notice we are standing along one of the high berm corners, out of sight of everyone.

Kade's hands are under my shirt spanning my waist, pulling my hips into his. His lips are at my neck, trailing his tongue up to my ear.

"Can I have you on the track, Cam?" he whispers with a very husky voice in my ear.

My knees begin to feel weak, my arms wrap tight around his neck, my fingers digging into his scalp at the back of his head. "

Someone can walk out here just like we did, Kade," I try with what very little sensibility I have left and even that is fading fast.

Kade trails his lips back down my neck as he is pushing me back a couple of steps. My shirt is now pulled up above my chest and I feel the coldness of the dirt when my back comes up against the solid wall. The coolness of the dirt rushes over my very hot body, the mixture of the two sensations is almost my doing alone. Kade's hands are now fisted around each side of my bra as he pulls it down over both my breasts, pushing them up to his lips. My head falls back against the dirt wall as his tongue takes turns circling around each nipple, then his mouth sucks one into it hard. My knees buckle under me, but Kade's knee is between my legs holding me up. I feel his hands now working on the button of my jeans, as I work on pulling his shirt up over his head and letting it drop to the ground. My hands run down his shoulders, his chest and I now work on getting the button of his jeans unfastened.

He slides the zipper of my jeans down and his fingers find what he is searching for. He rubs them against the very thin material of my panties. "Cam, you are already wet for me," without warning, he pushes them deep inside of me.

My back arches and the moan that tears from my chest I swear anyone around would be able to hear, but I couldn't care less of who is around now, all I want is Kade, deep inside of me.

He pulls his fingers from me and I want to scream out in protest, but before I can say anything my pants and remaining clothing is pushed down my legs and his tongue is now deep inside of me. My hands dig into his short hair as I thrust my hips into him, begging for so much more.

"Kade, please," I beg. I don't want to lose it in his mouth, I want him deep inside of me and right now I have no idea how much longer I can keep my release with him doing what he is with his tongue.

Grabbing his short hair, I pull his head away from me. His lips are instantly on mine. My hands work to push his pants and boxers over his legs. I feel his hardness against my hand and I wrap my fingers around him, stroking up and down the full, hard length of him. Taking his tip, I press it against my hot core and I hear a moan escape from both of us. Lightly I move my hips against him, taking him in just barely and with my hand still on him move him around that most sensitive spot I have. My head falls back and I feel that very familiar pulse starting.

Before I know what is happening he has me releasing him and spinning around, now my chest is pressed against the dirt wall. He spreads my legs as far as my jeans around my ankles will allow and then he thrusts in hard from behind me. Pushing my backside into him, I take him even deeper. He tries to start with a slow thrust but I don't allow it, I need this release and now, I can feel the vibration inside as it radiates up my belly and my breasts. My nipples even tingle right now.

Kade's hand comes around and his finger rubs over my sensitive bud and I'm gone. I know I yell out his name and couldn't at the moment care less if the whole damn party can hear. His hand comes up and he pinches my nipple and another wave of explosions happen.

"That's it, Cam, pull me deep inside of you." Kade's voice is husky and his breathing is deep as he speaks in my ear. He pinches once more and another wave rocks my body. His body goes stiff behind mine, his hips thrust hard against my backside and I swear I black out for a moment.

CHAPTER TWENTY-SIX

KADE

The track is empty this early in the morning, it's calm, quiet. In a couple hours it will be the complete opposite. You will hear the whining of the bikes' motors, the cheering of the fans, and the announcers over the speaker. It's amazing how quiet it can be right now, but this is my favorite time on the track, those few moments before the crazy begins.

This morning I woke up with Cammie curled up into my side and I realized how much my world has changed in just a couple short months. Fear spread through me like wildfire as I lay there and watched her sleep. Here was this amazing woman who took a chance on a playboy motocross rider and I have completely fallen in love with her. The fear is created by that love I feel. The responsibility that feeling Brookes with it is terrifying.

So this morning I decided to come to the one place my mind is always the clearest, this track. I left a note telling her where I would be, to catch a ride over with Cody and Krystal, and before I left I stood there by the bed for at least fifteen minutes staring down at her. How did one woman change everything so fast? The guys had warned me, but I of course laughed the off, but now I'm going to get the "I told you so" from each of them, because damn it, they were right.

I haven't been scared much in my life. Not even the highest jump or the largest blind curve has scared me, so why the hell can't I tell the woman that means the world to me that I love her?

The world behind me is starting to wake up, I can hear people talking, bikes being started up, the race is beginning and by the end of this weekend I will be the number one rider if I can keep my head on the track.

Walking back to the trailer, I go inside and start getting ready. I hear everyone as they arrive outside and when the trailer door opens there is Cammie. "Hey, I missed you this morning, everything all right?" She walks over and sits on my lap, bringing her head down and giving me a small kiss.

"Couldn't sleep, didn't want to wake you, so I came out here and did a little thinking."

"Nervous about the race?"

"About the race, no."

She searches my eyes for a moment, "Anything you need to talk about?"

Shaking my head, I bring her lips down to mine once more, and this time it's not just a sweet hello kiss, my tongue finds hers and she shifts in my lap. I need to keep kissing her so that my mouth doesn't spill the words I'm finding harder and harder to keep from saying.

When I look up at her again she has a puzzled look on her face. "Are you sure there isn't anything you need to talk about?"

Again, I nod. Standing up, she stands up with me and I grab my helmet that is sitting next to me. With a quick kiss on the forehead, I say, "Wish me luck."

"You don't need luck, you have this wrapped up for you pretty nice, just be careful, please." She looks up at me with a pleading in her eyes, but there is something else, almost like she is holding back something.

"Are you all right?" it's my turn to ask.

"I'll admit I always get a little nervous when you go out there, just be careful, please. I've seen that track from a whole new light."

Her eyes light up to that white-blue, which tells me she is talking about our little moment that we had on the track last night. "It will be a great reminder every time I pass that section of the track today."

"Keep your mind clear and your eyes open, please, no fantasizing on the track during a race," she scolds me.

"One more kiss for luck, and then I have to get going," I meet her lips and it's a soft kiss. When I open my eyes she is looking straight into mine. We both have something that needs to be said, but neither of us can say it yet. How is it I fear so much of telling her what I see reflected in her eyes?

"Good luck, be safe." She breaks the spell between us.

"You are my luck." I leave the trailer before either of us can say anything else.

LUCAS and my dad are standing with me at the lineup. Looking around, I spot Cammie. She is standing at the fence line just outside of the final turn, with a couple members of the crew and my mom. I can feel the tension in the air, this is the weekend that everyone has busted their asses to be at. My dad is saying something, but I'm able to tune him out with my helmet on and all the bikes revving around me. Lucas pats me on the shoulder. Looking over he gives me a thumbs up, I nod and the two of them back off behind me which signals that the race is about to begin.

We are halfway into the race, every time I've come around the corner my eyes land on Cammie and her smile beams. It's like we make eye contact for a split second, me letting her know I'm all good and her releasing the breath she is holding. My dad signals a good lead to me, but that doesn't mean I can get comfortable, this is when a couple of the guys start making their moves.

I'm almost to the halfway point of the track when I see the yellow flag go up, a crash has happened ahead. Slowing down, I look forward to keep an eye open on the track. Coming around the last corner I slow down, assuming this is the last spot for it to be, and there are a couple riders on the track and a group around them off to the side, but that's when I see the commotion over where the bystanders are watching, and right where Cammie was standing.

Slamming the brakes of my bike, it skids to a stop just outside of where my mom and Cammie were standing. I see a dirt bike laying on the ground and it looks like it went through the fence and that's all. Not sure what brings my eyes down to the ground but between the crowds, I somehow catch a glimpse of boots, cowboy boots actually, and they belong to one person. Pulling my helmet off, I throw it to the ground and run the few feet to where everyone is standing around. Two people are down on the ground —my mother, who is now sitting up next to my father, and Cammie, who is lying on the ground motionless.

Pushing through the mob of people, I finally make my way to her. Dropping on the ground, I go to reach for her and Lucas's hands fly up to stop me. "Don't move her, we don't know her injuries. The bike hit her, she may have neck or spine injury."

Everything around me seems to go in slow motion. I can see Lucas talking to me, but I can't hear a word he is saying. I need Cammie to know I am here, but everyone keeps pulling me back. "Everyone get your damn hands off of me," I finally find my voice.

"What the hell happened?" I ask, looking around at Lucas, then my dad, then my mom.

"The bike came flying over the barrier, it was heading straight for me, next thing I know, I'm being pushed and land on the ground. When I looked up Cammie was on the ground," my mom explains. My dad has her wrapped tight in his arms.

I want to wrap Cammie up in my arms and cradle her, tell her everything is going to be all right, but everyone keeps pulling me back. The event paramedics are here and all I can do is watch as they carefully place a neck brace on her and all together very gently and slowly they move her onto the stretcher. She hasn't moved a muscle, she hasn't made a sound.

In the distance I can hear the sound of the helicopter landing, I start to follow them and a young female paramedic holds me back. "I'm sorry, sir, no one else can fly with them. You can meet them over at Hope National."

Lucas is in front of me now, pushing me back from following, "Come on, Kade, we will meet them there."

Why is everyone pushing me away from her? It's starting to piss me off, next thing I know I'm taking a swing at one of my best friends. Not sure how he manages to duck so fast but I miss and the next thing I know my dad has my arms behind my back and is talking in my ear. "Kade, calm down. Come on, son, we need to get over to the hospital, but you need to pull it together."

They have loaded Cammie into the helicopter and have taken off in record time. I don't even remember getting into the truck, or even whose truck we are in, but I hear my dad on the phone with someone. His words are muffled in my head.

"She has no idea how I feel about her."

"Kade, she is a fighter, she is going to be fine and you will have plenty of time to tell her how you feel," Lucas reassures me. I didn't even know I had spoken my thoughts out loud.

It seems like it takes hours to get to the hospital. I'm jumping out even before the truck stops and running inside, straight to the nurses' desk, "Camille Mitchell, she was just brought in by helicopter, I need to know where she is."

The woman checks her computer, "Are you family?"

"Boyfriend, where is she?"

"If you will all have a seat, the doctor will be out shortly."

My fist slams down onto the station top, making the nurse jump. "I need you to let me see her now."

"Sorry," my dad's voice comes from behind me as he is pulling me away from the counter along with Lucas.

"Son, you aren't helping anything right now, sit down."

I don't think I have ever wanted to punch my dad as badly as I want to at this moment. Instead, I pull away from their grasp and walk back outside, I need some air.

Sitting down on the curb, I bury my face into my hands. Why didn't I tell her I loved her when we were out at the lake, or yesterday, or this morning? What if I don't get the chance to tell her? This was my fear. That crushing feeling I felt this morning when I lay there watching her sleep. It wasn't a fear of telling her I loved her, it was the fear of losing her. It can't hurt so much if you don't love someone, right? This was one of the reasons I stayed away from love, or relationships, it can't hurt if you don't feel it. Loving Cammie is easy, I'm pretty sure she even has the same feelings for me, it's in her eyes. So my fear hasn't been her not feeling the same, my fear has been losing her.

"Hey, man, you all right?" Lucas sits down beside me.

I shake my head no, "Why didn't you guys warn me about this part of falling in love? The fear part."

"Man, if you think Cammie doesn't love you..."

"No," I interrupt him, "I'm not afraid of her not loving me, I'm afraid of her not being here to love me."

"Kade, the doctor just came out and told us she is awake and talking. They have a couple more tests to run and they will be back out to tell us what is going on, but she is awake."

My heads hangs between my arms that are resting on my legs. I take a couple deep breaths and let Lucas's words soak in for a moment. She is awake and talking, which means she is going to make it through this. That's when I feel the tears on my cheek, I haven't cried since my grandmother died.

"Come on, let's get inside, so we know when the doctor comes back out," Lucas stands up and stretches out a hand to me. Grabbing it, he pulls me up off the curb.

"Sorry I took a swing at you earlier."

"Don't sweat it, you missed, I won't take it personally."

IT IS another hour before the doctor comes back out to the waiting room and fills us all in on Cammie's injuries. Broken collarbone, stitches in the shoulder, and some bruising on the face. Basically they are guessing when she pushed my mom out of the way, the bike skimmed her whole right side of her upper body. They are keeping her overnight for observation.

Opening the door to her room, I instantly hear the sound of the heart monitor. It almost brings me to my knees. She is alive and she is going to be all right. Poking my head around the corner, our eyes instantly connect.

"Hey," her voice is low and raspy, but the best sound I've heard all day.

Walking in, I don't even care to shut the door, I just need to touch her. Sitting down next to her, I take her hand into mine, bringing it to my lips and kissing her knuckles.

"Kade, I'm all right," her small voice is trying to reassure me.

"You were lying there so still, I thought I had lost you, Cam." I can feel the tears rolling down my cheeks and I couldn't care less, I've never been this scared and relieved in my life.

She lets go of my hand and brings her fingers up to my cheeks, brushing away my tears. "I'm just a little banged up, I'll be good and out of here in no time the doctor told me."

"You have no idea how much I love you."

CHAPTER TWENTY-SEVEN

CAMMIE

My hand freezes on his cheek, he turns his face, his lips now kissing the inside of my palm as he holds my hand. Did he just tell me he loves me?

"I should have told you days ago, or probably even weeks ago, but I'm not waiting anymore. Cam, I love you so much and the thought that I almost lost you today..."

"I love you, too, Kade." This feels right. We have had our moments where we both knew, but the words just weren't there yet, but here and now it's right.

"You have no idea how badly I want to be holding you right now."

"Can you at least get over here and give me a kiss, please?"

Standing up, his eyes roam over what I'm assuming are my injuries. It hurts to bring my hand up to his head but I don't care, pulling his head down to mine, our lips meet. "There isn't a day that is going to go by that I don't tell you I love you," his words are a whisper against my lips.

"Sounds good to me," I kiss him once more, then it hits me. "How did the race go? You had a great lead."

"I didn't finish the race."

"Wait, then that means you lose first place."

"Cammie, nothing is more important than being here with you."

"Kade, you worked too hard this year to be number one to give it up now. If you race tomorrow, do you still have a shot?"

"You are lying in a hospital bed, I just told you I love you and you are worried about what I place in the race?"

"That about sums it up, yes. Is there still a chance you can win?"

I can't allow him to just give it up now, if there is any chance for him to still have his dream of being number one he will be taking it, no matter where I am tomorrow.

"Yes, I would have to win tomorrow, but with my points already stacked up, today's race didn't knock me out of the running."

"Then you are racing."

"By the way, you saved my mom's life they say. That means I am forever in your debt."

"Isn't that supposed to go that she is forever in my debt?"

"Well I'm thinking I'll take on the challenge for her."

THE DOCTORS WON'T ALLOW Kade to stay the night, hospital policy, although Kade tries to use his charm to persuade a couple of the nurses and then blames me for losing his touch with the ladies, spouting off how falling in love with me has taken away his game.

The doctor does, however, come in early this morning and tells me they are releasing me. I make a phone call to Krystal and tell her to not say anything to Kade. I want to surprise him at the track. She and one other crew member come and pick me up around ten and even though the pain is almost unbearable, I can't miss his race.

They are just setting up on the starting line when I finally make it. Michael even has a special spot for me all set up in the announcer's booth. This has to be the best spot, I can see the whole track from here and there is no chance of flying motorcycles coming at me.

"Well, isn't this a sweet treat, we are honored to have our little hero from yesterday joining us up here in the box, Miss Camille Mitchell from the Sandy Racing Team."

Everyone in the stands turns to look up at the announcer's box cheering, but my eyes meet with Kade's very surprised ones. I want to be down there next to him, but this is where I was able to convince Michael I would be all right and he finally gave in, so at least I'm here.

"I love you," I mouth to Kade and even with his helmet on I can see his smile in his eyes.

Thirty minutes! Thirty of the longest minutes of my life it seems. I watch as Kade goes around each lap, gaining a little more distance from the rest of the riders each time he passes in front of us in the stands. There is no nail-biting story of him having to go neck and neck with another rider to keep his spot, he flies around that track like he is the only one on it.

Once the checkered flags go up, he makes his final jump over the last hill, drops his bike right there on the track and takes the stairs two or three at a time to get up to the announcer's booth, dropping his helmet somewhere on the way, I'm sure making a little kid's day, because if I know Kade he made sure it landed in some lucky kid's lap, the big softy.

As gentle as he can be with all the adrenaline rushing through him, he wraps an arm around my left side and pulls me into him for a victory kiss.

"Congratulations, you are number one. How does it feel?" I ask when he finally allows me up for some air.

"The only day that is going to compete is the day I marry you."

"Is that a proposal?"

"No, not yet, it will be done right. That's a promise!"

ABOUT THE AUTHOR

Tonya Clark lives in Southern California with her hot fire-fighter hubby and two daughters. She writes contemporary romance featuring second chance, sports, MC, shifters, suspense, and deaf culture-inspired by her youngest daughter.

When not hiding in the office writing, Tonya has the amazing job of photographing hot cover models, coaching multiple soccer teams, and running her day job.

Tonya believes everyone deserves their Happily Ever After!

Join Tonya's newsletter on her website: TonyaClarkBooks.com

instagram.com/authortonyaclark

bookbub.com/authors/tonya-clark

amazon.com/author/tonyaclark

goodreads.com/authortonyaclark

pinterest.com/mmcatcher75

facebook.com/authortonyaclark

ALSO BY TONYA CLARK

Sign of Love Series

Silent Burn

Silent Distraction

Silent Protection

Silent Forgiveness

Raven Boys Series (Written by Multiple Authors)

Entangled Rivals (Book 3 Can be read as a standalone)

Standalone

Retake

Driven Roads

Tell Me Goodbye (Coming Fall 2021)

Anthologies

Storybook Pub

Storybook Pub Christmas Wishes

Storybook Pub 2 (Coming June 2021)

Young Crush

Hate to Want You (Coming Sept 2021)